Dead Edit Redo

Dead Edit Redo

A Novella of Horror and Good Medicine

by
Elaine Stirling

Greyhart
Press

www.greyhartpress.com

⦿

"Come Upon Us Stealthily" by Abréu de Valletta, previously published in Poems from the Soles of His Feet, anthology translated, compiled and edited by Alain C. Dexter, Ph.D, Brougham College Press, © 2003.

"Let Me Be That Hand" by Alain C. Dexter, © 2008, reprinted with permission

"Unbreaking Fine Threads" and "Siege" appear in *Dead to Rights: A Circularity of Glosas*, 2nd edition, by Alain C. Dexter, © 2013

"Certain Things are Priceless" by Gavriel Navarro, © 2012, reprinted with permission

Hologram, A Book of Glosas by PK Page was published by Brick Books, London, Ontario, Canada, 1995

⦿

This book is a work of fiction, and all events have been imagined by the author. Occasional references to real people are used fictitiously. Any resemblence to actual events is coincidental and unintended.

To Dad and Mona

Come upon us stealthily

and find no less

than all the contents of

the treasure chests

of Solomon of which

you've never been

deprived, but for the

meagre state of thine

own mind.

—Abréu de Valletta, 1692

Contents

CHAPTER 1
SEVENTEEN, A PAIR OF PRIMES

Seventeen minutes ago, best-selling celebrity author and professor of poetry Alain C. Dexter posted the following note to his Facebook page:

I once knew a woman who
partied with dead poets. She
ate with them, she smoked and
drank and bargain hunted in their
company. Me, I wanted nothing more
than she, to marry her—she felt the same.
I lie. I wanted plenty more than she or her,
achieved it all, but she's not here. The one I
loved I never knew, and what I sought it
monstrous grew and now you are two
million strong, you like my page,
my posts are shared you click
and click—upon my word!
No matter how sublime
or rife with turd, this sad
poetic tweety bird. What flaps
before you now, my first authentic
scrip in seven years and ten, I do not
kid myself that you would recognize as
true if dithyrambed it did across your lawns
or sporked to graves of oceanic blue, this is my
last. The Tourbillon that spins, Valletta Falls
that drops shall be my space to versify, de-
grace in company of steelheads, young
sprats and bottom-feeding plaice.

Professor Dexter always included images with his Facebook notes, and this one was a photo of long, hairy toes protruding beyond the edge of a limestone outcrop. The background looked, at first glance, like blobs of shaving cream on a marble vanity, or Photoshopped thunderheads at twilight, but it was, in fact, the thrashing foam of white water rapids, thirty-six meters straight down. Within two minutes, his prose poem had received 659 likes and 93 comments, most of them hearts and smiley faces and variations on, "Edgy! Dark! Love it!!!"

A few of the comments would have made him laugh:

We used to picnic at Valletta Falls all the time when I was a kid. Enjoy!
Steelheads, cool!!! I luv Jamacian [sic] music!!!
Fishing is great therapy, Dr. A—wish I could be there, lol!

Eleven fans defriended Alain Dexter because they felt he had insulted them, and at Babar's, the Brougham College pub, a table of third year Enviro Sci students got into an argument with their Agric peers over steelheads. Are they salmon or trout? Apart from one reservations clerk in Borgarnes, Iceland, 2700 miles away, who happened to be a member of *Ásatrúarfélagið*, no one gave his post a second thought.

It was our first grown-up vacation, our first extended get-away that didn't involve leaky tents and inflatable mattresses. Eight days in a fishing cabin in the great Canadian north woods; eight days with no one but my best friend and lover Ginny Coulthard for company.

We had rented a cherry red, two-door Honda Civic from BCSU; we'd printed off road maps—for a laugh, mind you, as there was only one road to Hayden Lake and in some places only one lane, with right-of-way to logging trucks. We razzed each other about who was the more illustrious packer. For a pair of book nerds in pre-electronic reader days, it was a worthy debate.

"Your novels," Ginny contended, "are bulkier, but a single poem can blow a crater through impenetrable mass." She held up and waved a thin booklet worn to felt, and fringed with neon Post-its, while I hovered over my Brougham College gym bag, wondering whether Heinlein or Hardy would have to stay behind, to make room for my collapsible tripod.

"You can't bring Poe into this debate, Sugarbean," I said, reluctantly setting *Far From the Madding Crowd* aside.

"Why not?"

Because you always do, I nearly said, but apart from the book sacrifice, I was feeling chipper, so I didn't. I'd been sharing time, space and bed with Edgar Allan Poe since the day Ginny and I moved into our drafty co-ed dorm on the north shore of Lake Superior. She was writing her doctoral thesis on his final work, a 40,000 word prose poem called *Eureka*. What she and Poe believed to be his masterpiece, I viewed as a crock of self-aggrandizing pseudo-science, unworthy of a virtuoso of short horror fiction.

"Peppercorn," she said, "are you okay?"

I zipped the fake leather closed and eyed its bulging sides with distrust. "Sure. Why do you ask?"

"I don't know. It seems funny, I guess, you bringing a ton of books when you don't have to, and haven't you already read them all?"

"Yeah, but these are, or were, bestsellers in their day." I wrung my hands in parody of a mad scientist. "I intend to crack the code of their success, mwahahaha!"

She laughed and threw the car keys, ostensibly at me. I fished them from behind the stereo, and off we went.

Peppercorn and Sugarbean, those terms of endearment were goofy, and we didn't care.

At twenty-four, I was three years younger than Ginny. I had just slouched and cut-cornered my way through course requirements for an Honours B.A. in English Literature and intended never to write another essay or exam for as long as I lived. Ginny was fine with my ambition to become rich and famous. She loved academia with a zeal as fanatic as my resistance against it, and we were both fine with the idea of her working toward full professorship while I collected rejection slips en route to Alain C. Dexter, best-selling author.

My only rival for Sugarbean's affections did not enter our conversation again until the following afternoon when we were happily ensconced in our one-room log cabin at Hayden Lake. The cabin belonged to Brougham College as part of the legacy of the school's nineteenth-century founder and benefactor, Scottish-born lumber baron Archibald Brougham; it was rented out to students at a reasonable rate.

Our lakeside isolation was complete. We were surrounded by hundreds of square miles of dense coniferous woods. Until the logging road was cut in the late 1940s, Hayden Lake was accessible only by pontoon bush plane or canoe, the latter requiring torturous portages between river rapids, falls, and ancient aboriginal trails.

Ginny was working at the table near the window overlooking the lake. The night before, we had enjoyed barbecued chops, brown rice and salad on that scarred wooden table. So much for dining space. Now, it was buried under piles of spiral bound notebooks, textbooks and loose pages that surrounded her like a magic circle creeping outward from the table to the floor and the straight-back chair across from her.

"I think he intended to fail," she said.

"What?" I looked up from the trail guide where I was penciling notes on how to reach Valletta Falls.

"When Poe first shared *Eureka*. He must have known that people don't really want answers to the meaning of the universe."

"Don't they?"

I had claimed as my space the sinkhole in the middle of our saggy double bed. I sat propped by pillows against the brass headboard, within easy reach of a Heineken. Ginny sat with one bare heel on the chair, arms wrapped around her bare calf, chin resting on her knee. She wore the hemp bracelet with twin turquoise beads that I'd woven to prove I still had scouting skills on her slender, perfect ankle; the rope matched the shade of the gauzy cotton skirt that gathered at her thighs like the froth on a cappuccino.

"We don't," she said. "We want to know that we'll make it through the day safely, that whatever we perceive as encroaching and destructive doesn't come closer, and that what we desire, if we don't already have it, will sit still long enough for us to snatch and gobble before the next guy gets a chance."

"That is uncommonly cynical, Gin, even for you."

"I'm not being cynical, I'm placing myself in the mindset of Edgar Allen while he drew the guest list for his premiere reading. Listen, listen to his introduction." She read from her notes. "*I design to speak of the Physical, Metaphysical and Mathematical—of the Material and Spiritual Universe: of its Essence, its Origin, its Creation, its Present Condition and its Destiny.* You're a prose writer. You know how language works. What strikes you about that sentence?"

About halfway through Poe's words, which I envisioned as obsessively capitalized so that One Knew One Was Hearing Something Vitally Important, I had stopped listening. I asked her to read the quotation again.

She flared her nostrils, glared at me, and reread.

"Okay," I said. "It's first person, SVO, declarative. 'I design to speak of—he's owning it, no equivocation—followed by nicely organized specifics of what he intends to elaborate. Apart from sounding pompous—"

"Wait, wait, wait, why do you say pompous? If he'd said, I design to speak of the contents of my back yard—the leaves, the flowers, the insects, the dirt, would you have the same reaction?"

I knew I'd picked the wrong word even before Ginny dropped her bare foot to the floor. I'd sensed the oncoming collision with her 'listen, listen'; the triple 'wait' was a clincher. Poe had the masterful ability to engage our most primitive fear points, and any author worth his salt ought to study him, but as a person, I found him melodramatic; he displayed tendencies that today would be labeled obsessive-compulsive. He was a whiner, he nursed grudges; he droned on and on . . . sort of, like what I'm doing.

"No, I wouldn't react the same way about bugs and dirt," I said. "But he's claiming to know everything."

"About what?"

"Everything. No one likes people who claim omniscience."

"But he isn't, though. He didn't say, I claim knowledge of . . . he doesn't limit or discourage you from holding your own skill sets or beliefs—and this is my point. Poe invited the best thinkers of his day to a lecture in Buffalo—theologians, astronomers, mathematicians, classicists, physicians, hoping they would add their considerable portions to the sum of knowledge."

"Then that was his big mistake. You said as much yourself, we're all bullfrogs hunkered on our private lily pads, throwing out long curly tongues and competing for the best midges." I slapped a small biting something at the side of my neck.

"Exactly." She leaned forward, granting me an enticing view of braless, tank top cleavage. "That's where he gives the impression of having miscalculated, but Poe was a storyteller. He was a master of language and human nature in its full spectrum. He could have appealed to any of those groups individually—the scientists, the Spiritualists. Table rappers were on the upswing then, they'd have loved him, but instead he gathered a roomful of competitors and laid his entire system of understanding, in the gutsy form of satire, no less, at their spatted, patent-leather feet."

"And was rewarded with indifference of monumental proportions."

"So it would appear." She tapped a pen to her chin. "But you know the power of his stories. He could take readers anywhere he wanted, keep them up all night, turning pages—King, Koontz, all the great contemporaries, they take their hats off to him—and this is what I'm trying to develop in my thesis, that his fictional explorations ultimately led him to understand, maybe even interact with, levels of genuine omnipotence that underlie humanity. Poe believed—no, wrong word— he *saw* that all of us carry residual memory of our infinite nature. The concepts he introduced as radical, many now being proven through quantum mechanics, he regarded as our birthright. These powers are not something we have to earn or be taught." She drew quotation marks in the air to emphasize 'taught'. "Our chemical, biophysical, and energetic make-up source naturally from those levels of knowledge."

"Okay, your theory is out there, but I'm cool with it. But you still haven't explained why he chose to fail, as you put it. Why didn't he chase deep pockets of funding like any good artist or researcher?"

"Aha, pretty boy, now you're asking the right questions! He didn't chase funding because mammon, a.k.a. filthy lucre—poorly named, another trap—is a feature we've ascribed to an entropic insectoid activity that seeks to exclude, to compete, and Poe was throwing his *Eureka* further . . . to all of us, in the herenow." She lasered her baby blue-grays at me. "Do you hear what I'm saying, Alain? *All* of us."

God knows, I loved her intensity. God also knew that when she spiraled herself into one of those can't-you-hear-what-I'm-saying vortices, I became the dustballs and debris that blew away. I drained my Heineken with great solemnity and placed it on my sparsely-haired bare belly.

"Then he ought," I said, "to have rented a bigger hall."

She stared long enough to grasp that I was joking and mostly didn't care, then yowled and threw her pen at me. Fortunately, Ginny was the world's lousiest thrower, so my eyesight was never in danger. The blue-and-white striped Bic ricocheted off the headboard above me to fly across the room and hit the wallhanging behind the burgundy sofa, after which it ascended—which seemed a bit weird—and spun a few times before landing with a thud onto a fanned display of fishing magazines on the coffee table.

There was a knock on the door.

Chapter 2
Party Time

❧

Asti Fridleifsdotter was a member of *Ásatrúarfélagið*, the Icelandic neo-pagan group founded by farmer-poet Sveinbjörn Beinteinsson in 1972, but she didn't trouble herself much about that. For one thing, she'd had no say in the matter; her mother had added her to the roster the year she was born, 1993, and frankly, she found the robes and incantations a bit silly. Iceland was a nation that thrummed with nature gods, elves and ancestors; 40% of her citizens admitted to having experienced contact with the dead, and why shouldn't they? *Amma* talked to Asti all the time and may, once again, have contributed to the argument she'd had with her mother at their midday meal about attending a *blót*.

"Killing innocent animals will not put money in our bank account, Mother, and it won't bring you a boyfriend either!"

"Asti, we eat the animals. Animals give us protein." The daily post had arrived; Mother was scanning the envelopes and slapping them down. She glanced, lips pursed, over her reading glasses. "You could use some protein yourself. You're looking anemic."

You are not anemic, her grandmother said from the place in Asti's chest where she watched her daughter-in-law and criticized. *You're naturally pale like your father.*

"I'm vegan," Asti said, "and the smoke signals you send up are tainted with the innocent blood of sacrifice, and I will not be a part of it."

Mother removed her glasses and stared at Asti's open-faced sprout and tofu sandwich on stone-ground spelt. "I hope someone gave thanks to those soybeans before they sacrificed themselves to become fake salami."

And with that, she donned rubber boots and rain gear and clomped off with her fellow pagans to consecrate a barley field by decapitating a chicken. This left Asti blissfully *blót*-free at the reception desk of Birki

17

Skóga Inn, which had not a single guest, to surf the Internet. And to read the latest poem by Alain C. Dexter.

There, that's done, she heard *Amma* say.

He posted every day on Facebook. Some of his poetry was old and lame, but there was raw stuff too, untried and daring. A month ago, he'd held a contest for his million plus fans, inviting them to submit original poetry; the top prize was a signed, framed poem of one's choice. Even Mother had been thrilled when Asti won for her little poem, "With you, I am Fire". She'd selected Dexter's "Let Me Be That Hand" from an earlier collection of verse as her prize, and it hung in the lobby/café of the modest inn she and Mother ran together in Bogarnes, north of Reykjavik. It signed, *To Asti, for whom love and much happiness surely await, your Canadian friend, Alain. xoxo.* After Mother went to bed, Asti sometimes placed a lantern near the window and sat at the birchwood table with the blue flaxen placemats and imagined herself as the longed-for heroine of the poem.

But there was something wrong with the poem Alain Dexter had just posted. "I Once Knew a Woman" had appeared while Asti was scrolling the Newsfeed. She took in the title, read the opening lines and felt something cold and worm-like twisting between her breasts.

She clicked on the title to open the full poem. *Like, like, like, like, like*—she ignored the machine gun response of fans who couldn't have read something so complex so fast, and felt a whispering urgency—*there is no time, he has already done it! He has done it!*

Amma, what has he done?

But *Amma* didn't answer, and questions can be stalling tactics. Asti already knew what he had done—the squirming, writhing revulsion in her chest had told her, and if she didn't act now, if she allowed second thoughts to lumber in, the worst would play out its hand, the way it had when Father trudged with a coil of rope to the barn when Asti was three and—

NOOO!!!

She clicked to minimize the Facebook page and opened a Google window. In the search box, she typed in Tourbillon Valletta Falls Canada Police, and in 0.25 seconds, had the contact number for the

Ontario Provincial Police detachment in Nipigon on the north shore of Lake Superior.

How much it cost to phone halfway around the world, she neither knew nor cared. Using the hotel's landline, she punched the country code for Canada, followed by the ten numbers provided on the website. A male voice answered before the second ring: "OPP, Sergeant Belanger."

She spoke slowly and carefully in English. "Hello, my name is Asti Fridleifsdotter, and I wish to report an emergency."

❧◆❧

The five quick raps on the door stopped us both.

"Who the heck could that be?" Ginny asked.

Hayden Lake was four miles west of Highway 147 at the end of a twisty, pot-holed road that would rip out the muffler of anything traveling over fifteen miles an hour. The highway, if you looked at a map, shot arrow-straight northward, dead-ending at a patch of muskeg the size of Belgium where mosquitoes and black flies had, so far, fended off all attempts at logging, mining and other forms of human infestation; thirty-two miles to the south, it T-crossed with the coast-to-coast marvel known as the Trans-Canada Highway. Along its east-bound lane ran the rocky shore of Lake Superior, the stormiest, deepest and coldest of the legendary Great Lakes.

Brougham College, with 2400 or so students, sat nestled just north of the Trans-Canada behind a granite outcrop striated with rose quartz crystal that resembled an ocean liner's prow. The landmark had been named Mer de Rose by Francophone punsters. (Eliminate the space between r and d; if you still don't get it, Google translate.) Although the outcrop looked beautiful from the highway and in college brochures, it was, basically, an avian toilet with a view. The nearest town was Nipigon, twenty-two miles west of Mer de Rose.

I'm telling you all this so that you'll understand our little cabin with no telephone was a stone's throw beyond the tail end of the middle of nowhere, so when I said, "It's probably the hotel maid wanting to know if we'd like our sheets turned down," I was masking fear with irony.

The insistent rapping came again. We both jumped, and Ginny made a small whimpery noise.

"Alain, do we have a baseball bat or anything?"

"Not that I know of." I climbed off the bed to a squawk of rusty springs. "I didn't hear anyone drive up. Maybe they came from the lake."

I peered through the window nearest Ginny, then the one above the low brick and plank bookshelves near her side of the bed. The driveway ran alongside the cabin to a wooden boat launch at lake's edge. The two kayaks and canoe included in our rental fee were tied to the dock, undisturbed, and there were no other vessels. The only car visible in the driveway was our Honda.

Ginny got up from her chair, arms wrapped tightly around herself. "I bet it's the campus police." *With bad news*, she didn't have to say.

"You stay here. I'll deal with them." I patted her arm and crossed the single room of the cabin. We'd locked the inside door with the deadbolt because northern Ontario is bear country, and bears can turn door knobs. The screen door, I hoped, was latched.

I pushed back the orange and brown plaid curtain on the small window. Two men stood on the porch. An enormous rifle rested on the shoulder of the shorter man; the other carried a clay jug.

"Who is it?" Ginny had come as far as the kitchenette, about halfway.

"I don't know. Stay there. I've never seen them before."

The armed man caught my eye and lifted what appeared, upon closer inspection, to be a flintlock musket. He shook it up and down in a half-obscene gesture while grinning, wide-eyed and maniacal. "*Bonjour, bonjour*," he shouted through both doors. "*J'espère que nous ne sommes pas trop tard.*"

As it happens, I was born and raised in what we call the Soo, Sault Ste. Marie, Ontario, a former steel town on St. Mary's River between Lake Superior and Lake Huron. My mother was Quebecois, and I'd retained enough of my cradle tongue to understand the strangely accented French.

"*Je ne parle pas Francais,*" I fibbed. "I think you have the wrong house."

He looked at his tall, gaunt companion who shrugged. The Frenchman was small, leathery and bright-eyed like a river otter. He spoke a word that to the ear unaccustomed to Canadian French sounds like a duck with sinus trouble.

"*Quoi?*"

I repeated what I'd said, more loudly. They were probably woodsmen, I decided, who'd run into trouble on a portage.

"But dat cannot be," the man said, switching to patois English. "Da party, it's here, *non?*"

His friend, as if to confirm the fact, waggled his eyebrows and held up the large clay jug by its ear.

"Why do they think we're having a party?" Ginny asked. She stood six feet away from the door and had spoken in her inside voice.

The man's face lit up. "*Aah, la p'ti' belle! Elle est ici!*" He shook his musket again in that disturbing way, which made me wish I had something that looked semi-automatic. He pressed his face into the screen door. "*Bonjour, mon amour, comme t'allez vous?*"

I shoved a finger at him, gun-like, at nose level. "You back off right now, before I call the police."

The tall man spoke for the first time. "There's no phone in the cabin. How are you planning to do that?"

"I have a cell. Gin, call 9-1-1."

"But we don't—" Catching on, she stopped herself. "Okay, I'm calling," she said, curling a palm and punching imaginary numbers.

"You have a what?" The man's English was not only free of Quebecois twang, he pronounced 'what' in the two-syllable, upper middle class fashion—*hoo-what?*

"A mobile, a cell phone."

"Yes, I'd like to report a trespass at Hayden Lake," Ginny said loudly to her palm, cupped at her right ear.

"Trespass?" The man laughed. "Now, that's rich."

"Who are you?" I said, my fear morphing to impatience. "We're paid up for eight days. I have the receipt."

He had the audacity to open the screen door—so it wasn't latched—and prop it defiantly behind him. He wore a red and black plaid hunting jacket; his dark hair was longish and pompadoured like Rizzo from *Grease*.

"You didn't pay me," he said.

"And who are you?"

"Hah!" The Frenchman lifted his thigh and slapped it as if I'd ripped a good one. "You don' know 'oo he is, dis man?"

"I don't know either of you. Why should I?"

"Because we're famous, aren't we, 'ayden? At least, you are—me, I'm nobody."

Aiden—no, Hayden; the French drop their haitches. Inner wheels started turning. I knew his story; drunked variations of it got told at every college bonfire. Hayden Lake was named after the son of the benefactor who bequeathed grounds, buildings and money to found Brougham College upon his death. He was, if I recalled correctly, Archibald Brougham's only son, born to his first wife, Susannah, who came with him from Scotland in the late 1800's.

Local lore had it that Hayden Brougham—the original, obviously, not this guy—drowned in the lake that now bore his name. He'd wanted to be a writer like Jack London, and while he had the connections and maybe even talent, some weakness in his character prevented Hayden from attaining his goals. The seclusion he sought here in the north woods became reclusiveness; he drank, smoked opium and jimweed, smuggled to him by a complicated network of trappers, fishermen and dissolute priests. He wrote of hallucinations so terrifying his father arranged to have him committed to an insane asylum in southern Ontario. In late spring, 1917—right around this time of year—the white coats arrived in a Curtis HS-2L, the newly designed twin-engined flying boat hired at enormous cost from Curtis Aircraft in Buffalo, New York. But when the American bush pilot landed on the lake, they found Hayden Brougham floating face down, his canoe and paddles undisturbed nearby. On the floor of the canoe, they found a notebook, an empty fifth of brandy, and a broken pencil. He was twenty-four . . . same age as me.

Curiosity had, by now, overcome Ginny. She peered through the window and turned to me. "We're being rude, talking to these gentlemen through the door."

"They are not gentlemen," I said, feeling the creeping heat of rudeness. "We don't even kn—"

"Here, put this on." She handed me my long-sleeved cambric shirt and before I could stop her, she elbowed me aside and unbolted the door. The man named Hayden stepped back to make room for her on the porch. "I'm Ginny Coulthard. This is my boyfriend, Alain Dexter."

"How do you do? I'm Hayden Brougham."

Standing behind Ginny, I watched them shake hands; she turned and with a fierce look, urged me to do the same. Brougham's handshake was firm, the skin calloused as one would expect from someone who canoed and chopped wood.

"And this," Hayden said, "is my friend, Abréu de Valletta. He's a poet, Miss Coulthard, like you."

The hairs on the back of my neck rose. Not only because a tall, dark-haired—and yeah, I guess, you'd say handsome—stranger knew that my girlfriend wrote poetry, but because the man he'd introduced as Abréu de Valletta had leaned his flintlock against the cabin wall and was bending over to kiss Ginny's hand with a ridiculous flourish of his free arm, which made her blush and giggle. And because the coarse linen shirt and leather breeches of the Frenchman, if that's what he was, appeared, well, of its time—like a seventeenth century *voyageur*. He smelled of bear grease. Now, I had done some acting in my day; I knew the importance of attention to costume detail, and while it wasn't unheard of for contemporary outdoorsmen to employ traditional bug repellants, I wasn't liking the overall sum of things.

"So what's this about a party?" Ginny said, after I'd grudgingly shaken Abréu's hand and wiped the grease off on my jeans.

Why was his name sticking in my craw?

Because it was fake. Just like Hayden Brougham's name was fake. Valletta Falls was a nearby landmark, downstream from the Tourbillon River that flowed out of Hayden Lake, itself receiving water from an underground stream. I'd been studying the trails and canoe routes just before these guys arrived. The coincidences were untenable, in the same way that—I struggled for analogy, but my brain was feeling muddled, and were those tiny golden sparks I saw flying off Ginny? My brain rejected that last detail and gave me an analogy for why this whole thing was impossible: it would be like meeting a guy in velvet cape and buckled shoes named Walt Raleigh at a tobacconist's in North Carolina.

I wondered if I was having an aneurysm.

"I know you've rented my place," the so-called Hayden said, "and we wouldn't dream of imposing, but Edgar said he had okayed it with you—and well, the others will be coming soon. I brought wine."

Ginny swayed a little and hooked a hand around my biceps. "Edgar?" she said.

"Mm-hm, here." He reached into an inner pocket of his hunting jacket.

Abréu, I could see from the corner of my eye, was watching me watch Hayden; his mouth twitched as if he could barely keep from laughing. Couldn't stay in character, obviously. I placed my hand over Ginny's and felt the sweet, solid anchor of her.

"It's not a first edition or anything, although I think in Dad's archives, there may be one." Hayden pulled out a light gray booklet, worn to soft felt, identical, except for the absence of neon Post-its, to Ginny's copy of Edgar Allan Poe's *Eureka*.

⁓◦❦◦⁓

Constable Elsie Kalahash of the Ontario Provincial Police, Nipigon Detachment, was running late. They used to call that sort of thing with people like her "Indian time", but that was before the era of cultural sensitivity training for Canada's public service sectors. Staff Sergeant Ernie Bartelli called her "squaw" once, but he was drunk and he'd just lost his wife to early onset Parkinson's. As a card-carrying member of the Maškēkowak or Swampy Cree First Nation, Elsie had heard and, in her younger days, avenged much worse.

She was running late because Constable First Class Tom Edgewell hated paperwork, and he didn't trust computers, and apart from a few speeders on the Trans-Canada and a domestic, things had been quiet on the 3-11, so he didn't figure she'd mind filing the incident reports on the graveyard shift, which he figured would be equally quiet. It was all there in the log. And she was running late because the staff refrigerator hadn't been emptied or cleaned, probably since Y2K, and new recycling standards required that Tupperware and other plastic containers that bulged and pulsed with green-grayish furry goo be washed prior to Blue Boxing them. Arranging office fans to keep the stench blowing away from workspace areas, running outside to dry heave, and to argue with Staff Sergeant Bartelli who thought she should just drive the whole lot to the dump—bears'll eat anything—took time.

At 7:47 a.m., nearly an hour into her four days off, Elsie phoned Little Sister Jenah-Rae on her mobile. Her dad's voicemail picked up. "You have reached the Chappell residence. We are not able to take your call right now . . ."

"Hey, Jen, it's Elsie. I'm just leaving work now. Going home to pick up the truck. I'll be there in twenty. Don't forget to eat breakfast."

The thought of food made Elsie queasy, but she poured herself a mug of amber-coloured sun tea from the four-litre jar she kept near the staff kitchen window. It was her grandmother's traditional recipe, made of dried sage and wild thyme, and none of her colleagues, being addicted to tarry black sludge with non-dairy creamer in the manner of cops everywhere, went near the stuff.

Sergeant Howie Belanger, a sixteen-year veteran who'd just come on for the day shift, threw a pre-measured filter pack into the drip machine, looked at her with a flat expression, and said, "You still here?"

She leaned against the file cabinet that doubled as a condiment shelf and sipped the cool tea unhurriedly. "Not for much longer."

Belanger, in her opinion, was one of those borderline cops who could just as easily have chosen a career in petty thievery as law enforcement. A month ago, he had drawn a hazmat symbol and printed Cree Pee in permanent black marker on the tea jar. She'd known right away who did it. You don't grow up on the streets of North Winnipeg, bouncing from one well-meaning but disastrous foster home to another, without a keenly developed sixth sense. What bothered her more than the blatant ignorance of the act was her own blinding rage when she saw it. If Belanger had been on duty at the time, she might have over-ridden her own twelve years of active OPP duty, ignored the wall full of certificates in anger management courses—both First Nations and the white man's—that she'd not only completed but facilitated, and pistol-whipped his acne-pitted face to pulp.

The only thing that stopped her were the Medicine Wheels she had painted with full ceremony by an artist elder on both rear side panels of her Vespa GTV 300. You don't defeat the spirit of the West by adding to its energy. And so she'd taken sweetgrass out behind the detachment, offered prayers to the seven directions and smudged away her anger.

Her colleagues, most of whom were decent men and women, hadn't find Belanger's vandalism funny, at least not to Elsie's face, but no one would admit to knowing, or even suspecting, who did it either. She took her certainty alone to the Staff Sergeant who feared ministerial inquiry enough that he didn't insist that she brush it off as a harmless prank. By means she never learned, he extracted a confession from Sergeant Belanger and ordered him to scrub the jar clean and offer an apology in writing to Elsie. Things had been uncomfortable between them ever since.

The coffee machine dribbled and gurgled and belched steam while Sgt. Belanger dropped two rounded spoonfuls of Coffee-Mate into his Bud's Esso Curling mug. Elsie swirled the final two sips of sun tea around in her mouth and took shameless pleasure in following his every move.

And then the phone rang.

Constable Darla Whitefish, Belanger's partner on the day shift, was in the ladies' room, and Elsie, of course, was already off duty. Belanger had no choice but to leave the staff room and take the call.

"Nipigon OPP, Sergeant Belanger."

Elsie rinsed out the Garfield mug she'd received from Jenah-Rae last Christmas, towel dried and placed it in the cupboard above the sink.

"What kind of emergency? Where are you calling from?" Belanger, whose ordinary telephone voice rattled blinds, ramped the volume. "From *where?*" Elsie stepped out into the public area in time to hear him bellow, "Iceland! Is that the big island off Newfoundland, all snowy?"

She bit her upper lip and kept her face turned away while passing his desk to the lockers, where she quietly removed her backpack and jacket.

"That's a very strange thing you're telling me, Ma'am."

Darla came out of the ladies' room and cast a curious glance toward Elsie, who responded with a shrug and a grin. They were sharing the same ungracious thought: Iceland is far away, so you have to really shout loud.

"Well, yes, Valletta Falls is our juris—no, we're not on Facebook, Ma'am."

Darla went to her work station at the front desk and squirted a few drops of sanitizer on her hands, a quiet enough activity to allow for eavesdropping. The corridor with lockers was behind Belanger's desk, so he couldn't see Elsie listening in too.

"Yes, we have computers and Internet access, but we don't generally accept emails from unknown urls, Ma'am, especially not with links or attachments. We have firewalls . . . yes, I'm sure Facebook is virus-free, but why do you have reason to—"

A high-pitched tone, more vibration than voice, caught Elsie's ear and ran like lightning bolts down the length of her body and out both arms and legs. The distress of the woman at the other end was bypassing Belanger because he wasn't listening, and her agitation had to ground itself somewhere. It was basic Swampy Cree logic. Constable Whitefish, in that same instant, came to a seated attention. Elsie watched her log onto Google at her desktop and, typing swiftly, log onto her personal Facebook account. Those were the last ordinary movements Elsie absorbed before another kind of knowing—one that predated Winnipeg and the foster homes and her mother's crystal meth addiction that led to her murder when Elsie was two—took over.

The air around her turned buoyant, like marshmallow clouds. She walked toward Sgt. Belanger's workspace on her own two legs, and yet it felt more like distance was rolling in on itself, and that he was spooling toward her. Elsie lifted his straight-back gray padded visitor chair and repositioned it so that she could sit beside Belanger, to his left. She sank into the chair with that same floating sensation.

He gave her a curious look and leaned away from her in the way that school kids used to with an accompanying, "Yieuww, I don't want Indian cooties," but though she could see several layers into his sophomoric thought processes and none were impressive, she ignored them and picked up a battered OPP field notebook from his Inbox.

Darla's on Facebook, she wrote quickly, abandoning rank and file protocol. *Ask caller to send link as private msg to Fishing Derby Queen.*

"Erm . . . um, Ma'am?" Belanger tipped his head to read Elsie's note. "If you'll send that link to . . . Fishing Derby Queen—" He pronounced each word separately and awkwardly as if they were new to him. "—yes, that's right, D-E-R-B-Y."

He gave Elsie a slightly panicked look. *What now?* She pointed toward Darla who gave them a hasty thumbs up while moving from the Facebook Newsfeed page to Messages.

"I've got it," said Constable Whitefish. "A message from Asti . . ." She moved closer to the screen. "Frid . . . leifs . . . dotter. There's a link to a fan page. Alain C. Dexter."

"Put her on speaker, Sir." Elsie got up and turned on the printer that was shared by all desktops in the open area. "Tell her we've received the message."

Constable Belanger followed her instructions.

"Hello, Ma'am," Elsie said. "I hope I can call you Asti. My name is Elsie Kalahash, I'm a Constable First Class and I'm here with Sgt. Belanger whom you've been speaking to, along with Constable Darla Whitefish." A rookie with only two years on the force but who consistently showed all the heart and promise of an exemplary police officer.

"Thank you," Darla mouthed with a slight flush to her cheeks, as if Elsie's commendation had been spoken aloud. She hit a few keys, and the printer across the room growled to life.

"Do you know where is Valletta Falls?" said the young lilting female voice from Iceland.

"I know the area very well," Elsie said, sidling to the printer. "Three copies, please, Darla. The page you've sent us is coming out now, Asti . . . It's a . . . I can see it's a—" She wanted to say, a pair of women's breasts, but the document was only words—a poem—that had been shaped to symbolize breasts. Budget cuts didn't allow for a colour printer outside the Staff Sergeant's office—never mind that new printer/copier/scanners were cheaper than the black-only toner for this clunker. Still, Elsie recognized the photo of the Tourbillon River that accompanied the poem, "I Once Knew a Woman" that she was now distributing to her colleagues.

If Alain C. Dexter, who was apparently famous, based on the number of likes and comments, took the photo at the same time that he'd posted the Note, seven minutes ago, and if he'd done what every cell in her body was screaming in high-pitched, eerily calm unison he had done, then he couldn't have picked a more efficient place to do it.

Elsie knew her next move. In that same instant, Sgt. Belanger reverted to his thick-as-a-plank, dick-headed-but-cop-nonetheless self and said, "Ma'am, I am sorry to say we do not have sufficient grounds to take action in this situation. Nowhere in this document do I see—"

"But it's everywhere on the document, Officer!" argued the feisty Icelander for whom Elsie accorded full points for following intuition and the voice of her elders.

Belanger mowed right over her insistence with, "Now, if a member of his family were to contact us and report him missing—"

Elsie didn't wait to hear more. She tapped Darla on the shoulder in a gesture of thanks and solidarity and rushed out of the detachment. With one hand, she threw her backpack and jacket into the storage compartment of her turquoise blue Vespa; with the other, she thumb-dialed the number for Jenah-Rae, her Little Sister, who answered (thank you, Great Spirit!) on the first ring.

"There's been a change of plans, Jenah. Can you be ready and waiting outside in three minutes?" She straddled the Vespa, turned on the ignition.

"Um, yeah . . .?" she replied in the guarded tone of a thirteen-year-old.

Elsie peeled out of the Nipigon OPP detachment in a spray of gravel and puddles from last night's rain. "Wear long pants, bring a jacket and lots of bug spray."

CHAPTER 3

"DIS HERE'S DA TIRD PLACE."

Guests began to arrive at the party in our little cabin at Hayden Lake while my back was turned—a detail that you ought to view with suspicion, as there was only one door and I was facing it.

Still sorting things out, I was less than pleased with Ginny's precipitous decision to allow two strangers—men—to intrude on our privacy. The one who claimed to be Hayden Brougham, son of the founder of Brougham College, had the loose-boned slouch typical of certain tall guys who can snag women simply by looking hung over and rumpled. He carried his enormous jug of hooch on one shoulder with an index finger hooked into the ear, and I made a mental note to warn Ginny not to touch whatever he poured from it. He walked in like he owned the place, which, eighty years ago, he had.

The little guy, Abréu de Valletta, now there was a cracker. He stood scarcely five feet tall and was so bowlegged, so rigid at the hips, he looked like a cross between a human and a croquet wicket. He beetle-hopped inside and placed his flintlock musket, which I still believed to be a prop or I would never have let him bring it inside, carefully in the nearest corner. He then sidled to the door frame, grabbed hold of it with his left hand, pulled himself up on tiptoe, and rested his forehead a moment against an object I had not noticed before.

He turned to me and said, "Every tird place should have protection."

"Turd place?" I said, truly not intending to make fun of his accent. I looked at the small ceramic tube nailed to the door frame. Had a mezuzah, symbol of God's protection for Orthodox Jews, always been there?

"My Uncle Shabtai-Tzvi, before they tied him in a sack and sent him to Albania disguised as potatoes, always talked about the tird place. Me, I tink he got stuck there, den things came out his mouth, they sound so holy, people start thinkin' he's the Messiah." Abréu threw his arm up, made a *pffft* sound and pushed past me. "He was a poet, a madman like the rest of us."

Oh, third place! That's what he'd said. All the rest was gibberish.

At this point, I turned around, and my first thought was, where did all these people come from? But then something lateral and fluid picked up the question and whooshed it downstream like those flash floods that turn dusty streets into torrents, and my next concern, which felt much more comfortable, even rational, was, I hope there'll be enough places for everyone to sit; then the hope itself seemed absurd, as if I were worried about sufficient oxygen to go around.

Ginny seemed to be at the center of the flow of the mingling guests, whose numbers ranged from eight to twelve to twenty and back down to—it was impossible to count them. No one stood still long enough, or rather, they stood in typical cocktail party clusters, but not consistently; they came, they went, they appeared and non-appeared. Ginny, thank heavens, remained substantial enough and looked happy as a clam.

She stood beside the coffee table in front of the sofa where moments ago her ball point pen had landed. The pen was still there, on top of the fanned fishing magazines—that detail felt particularly assuring—and she was conversing with a curly-haired, fine-boned man who wore a ruffled shirt open at the chest and who stood close when he talked to her. Another man in the kind of spectacles John Lennon would make fashionable centuries later, was examining the wall hanging behind the couch. I hadn't paid much attention to it: a circular frame, divided into quadrants, wrapped in leather twine with four garishly dyed feathers hanging from it. It was typical kitsch, a dream catcher, I don't know, the kind one found in souvenir shops, what we call trading posts along this stretch of the Trans-Canada.

He removed his glasses and turned to ask a question of a stocky, bronze, bare-chested man with a ring through his nose who reminded me of Yul Brynner in *The King and I*—and why were there so few women at this party?

"Epictetus. You should feel honoured. He doesn't often show up at these soirées."

"I beg your pardon?" I turned to find an elegant woman with large expressive eyes, forearm propped with her opposite hand, regarding me with amusement through a wisp of cigarette smoke. Her tightly tailored tweed suit looked expensive and a few decades out-of-style. I guessed she'd be in her early fifties, about my mother's age.

"That's about right," she said, as if I'd conjectured aloud. She held out the hand that didn't hold the cigarette. "P.K. Page. You may call me Patricia."

"Alain Dexter, pleased to meet you." A thousand questions were trampling to be first out of the gate, and in these situations, the cleverest one doesn't always win. "So this is a soirée, is it?"

To my ears, I sounded abysmally red-neck, which I'm not, in the technical sense of the word. I mean, I did possess an English Lit. degree, fresh off the presses, and I knew, in an academic sense, that Epictetus had been a Stoic philosopher before the time of Christ, and whose real name was unknown. Epictetus meant "owned".

Patricia had a lovely smile that crinkled and relaxed her heart-shaped face. "Something like that. Why don't we go over to the sofa before someone else snags it? I'm sure we'll have much to talk about."

Though I trusted her as much as one can trust anything in a hallucinatory state, I found myself as we headed toward the sofa searching for Hayden and Abréu, who were surely the instigators. Searching a space no larger than 20 by 40 feet ought not to have posed much of a challenge, but the cracker box dimensions seemed to wow in and out in the way things do when an opthalmologist puts dilating drops in your eyes. I spied Hayden in the overstuffed upholstered chair with a woman on his lap—who, thank God, was not Ginny—and where was all this possessiveness coming from? The woman had waist-length red ringlets, a few shades darker than my own unruly mop and a skirt made of leather strips that exposed taut, slender thighs pretty much all the way up to where thighs end. Abréu sat on the small kitchen counter with one of my Heinekens resting between his bow legs, deep in conversation with . . . and here I had to pause because my acutely over-strained rationality wanted to say, in regard to the turbaned man in floral silk with pointy-toed slippers: Rumi.

Patricia's laughter was hearty and bell-like. "Well done," she said, sitting in the center of the sofa. "The first time this happened to me, I clamped down my recognition skills so hard that the waffle iron shorted. Not that Arthur, my husband, connected the two events. He was a diplomat, and he just wanted his breakfast."

"So you can read my thoughts," I said.

"Of course not." She smoothed her skirt over silk-stockinged knees. "What I heard was—'look at that little bastard, drinking my beer, and holy'—you used an expletive—'that's Rumi'. And indeed, he is. They were the first, you know, the Turks, the Persians, to identify the third place. Of course, back then, you didn't dare to call yourself a mathematician or astronomer if you weren't well practiced in poetry." She leaned forward and seemed especially interested in the pen lying on the coffee table.

"Did they . . . um, had ball points not been invented yet when you, um . . . .?" I was trying hard to get into this game, but I had so few points of reference.

She laughed again. "Wrote poetry? Yes, this version of me is considerably more youthful than what you might observe at, say . . . a Brougham College reading, but I am familiar with recent advancements in writing implements. What had me curious and not a little flattered is what your lovely fiancée's pen is pointing to."

Ginny and I were not yet engaged, but I was slowly starting to absorb the fact that we could be, would be, and might become engaged at some point further down from this . . . erm, point. Was the pen pointing at something? Why had Ginny thrown it? Something about Poe's *Eureka*. Where was Edgar Allan? Shouldn't he be here? Look at that, I was getting into the game!

Patricia, with a red-laquered fingernail, lifted the top two fishing magazines from the stack and pulled out an ocher yellow, magazine-sized, softcover book. With the casual grace of an experienced wordsmith, she picked up the pen and opened to the inside title page that would eventually, almost of its own accord, sum up everything:

Hologram
A Book of Glosas
P K Page

"Oh, look," she said. "Milton has arrived, and of course, he makes a beeline toward the prettiest face. Now, shall I inscribe this to both of you?"

❧❦❧

"Tell me again why we're giving up premium camping space at Pukaskwa on a long weekend that we've been planning for a year?"

Elsie Kalahash rolled the Vespa into a narrow shady space between two juniper bushes, surrounded by tall pines. With the toe of her soft-soled moccasin, she lowered the kickstand. "We're not giving up anything. I've confirmed the space on credit card, and I never told you why in the first place. You're bluffing, Little Mynx."

Jenna-Rae giggled as she removed and stowed her motorcycle helmet. "Is the alarm off?"

"It is, thank you for asking."

Even if they'd parked at the official entrance to Valletta Falls Provincial Park instead of taking back trails into deep bush where no four-wheeled vehicle could enter, she'd have disengaged the anti-theft siren. There would be no electronic screeching to frighten the four-legged, the creeping and the flying nations.

Jenah gathered leafy deadwood and brushed the boughs lightly across the scooter, softly chanting thanksgiving and protection songs. She was in sync with All That Is, and it filled Elsie's heart to watch.

Elsie had given Jenah-Rae her Maškēkowak name, Little Mynx, when they first became Big Sister/Little Sister, eight years ago. Jenah, adopted as an infant by Doug and Marie Chappell, was one-quarter Haida First Nation, one-quarter Chinese, and one-half indeterminate Caribbean. She had just lost her adoptive mom to breast cancer. Three years later, her dad, a gentle soul, a carpenter, lost his job in the 2007 fire that destroyed Nipigon's wood products factory, the town's main employer. Doug Chappell scratched a living from home renos and repairs and might even have thrived in a city where people have lost their hand skills, but the sour smoke that blinds—depression, in white man's jargon—kept him most days watching cable sports with the curtains drawn.

"Where's your Deet?" Elsie asked.

Jenah pulled the non-aerosol repellant from her jacket pocket. "I don't think I need it. I hardly get bitten at all anymore."

"That's because town mosquitoes have manners, and they know you. Where we're going, there'll be creatures who've never tasted sweet young human. Cover your eyes, turn."

Elsie would use no white man's medicine on herself today. Whatever might be attracted enough to bite or investigate would also bring information about the man at Valletta Falls. As any good cop knows, you don't scare off informants.

She tucked the repellant back into the girl's pocket and gave her a quick scan. Jenah-Rae was tall for her age with shoulder-length ebony corkscrew curls and a sleek angular bone structure that gave her the movement and grace of a feline hunter. She was also remarkably— unlike Elsie, who battled it in one form or another every day—free of anger.

"Okay, so here's the deal," Elsie said. "We walk one behind the other, Indian-style. The route we're taking to Valletta, there is no visible trail. We make the trail by opening our hearts, by showing the nations of the creeping, flying and four-leggeds that we mean no harm. Do you understand?"

"Lips zipped," Jenah said, with a horizontal swipe across her mouth.

"That's right, and because you are mynx in training, you'll imitate my trail. You know how to walk Cree, outside of soles first, roll inward. The cushion of your feet, cushion of Mother Earth, let them be the same."

Jenah listened, wide-eyed; she looked down at her white Nikes with green racing stripes and practiced with left foot, then right to make the steps with no sound.

With every syllable of instruction, Elsie Kalahash felt more and more of the bindings of *wasichu*, white man, fall away. What made her a half-decent cop, if revealed in full colour, would throw her off the provincial payroll faster than lightning hits dead pine, and that was okay. The laws that bind water, rocks, sky, trees, earth, and animals are the same laws that bind humanity; she didn't have to become something different than herself in the deep woods, only something truer . . .

Elsie was fourteen when she was delivered by bush plane to Innis Landing on the southwest shore of Hudson Bay, wrapped in two sleeping bags, one inside the other, that had been donated by St. Vincent de Paul. Jimmy Small Beaver, twenty-three years later, still loved to tell the story of how he rolled her up in bungee cord and threw her into the household items bin. That's how little substance there was of her. If the pilot, Ed O'Neill, hadn't been offloading cases of Orange Crush and Diet Coke and seen him do it, well—stories like that made people laugh, and laughter made good medicine.

She had been drunk and high on coke, pot and meth for months, partying in the crack houses and frigid back allies of Winnipeg. Once in a while, she dropped in to the Indian Friendship Centre for a coffee or a bus ticket that she'd trade for cash; but in those final days, dehydrated and malnourished, her body rejected food and nonalcoholic fluids, even water, with vomiting and petit mal seizures. She had no conscious memory of the miscarriage at sixteen weeks, the result of a gang rape behind a dumpster at a strip mall. She'd been partied hard before, but not in such a weakened state that she couldn't fight off the broken bottles, cigarette burns and switch blades. That she'd conceived and carried a fetus for as long as she did would have defied modern medicine, had she seen a doctor, but in the end, it was the hemorrhaging that rendered her permanently infertile and nearly killed her that cold night in March.

Bleeding, with her blood pressure and vital signs falling away, she crawled on her belly and forearms from the back door of a pawn shop on Selkirk Avenue that she'd been trying to break into. For over a mile, she creeped and scraped and pulled herself across gravel, asphalt, ice, and snow like a worm. No thoughts ran through her, she held no destination in mind, only a direction, southeast, and she maintained it, deviating without hesitation around parked cars and other obstacles; waiting at curbs, gaze lowered, invisible, while traffic roared by. On one occasion, she miscalculated and was nearly run over by a newspaper truck; the driver swerved but didn't honk because she looked a piece of blown debris, nothing to get angry at. Elsie lay draped across the boulevard median until she'd recovered her will. In the dawn twilight, she reached the fork of the Red and the Assiniboine Rivers, and her body stopped.

For millennia, the rolling landscape at the juncture of the two waterways had been a sacred place of gathering to the tribes or First Nations of Canada. Later, the railroads moved in and more recently the yuppies, but on that night of -10 Celsius, mild for Winnipeg in March, when Elsie reached the frozen muddy bank of the Red River where it flowed underneath the St. Boniface Bridge, there were no paved walkways, no fancy waterfront restaurants, patios and terraces. Two constables on the unpopular beat of picking up passed out, frozen or dead aboriginals along the river banks found Elsie lying face down, mid-river, on snow-covered ice, with a dwindling trail of blood and claw-like scrape marks where she'd tried to dig her way into the water.

They phoned for an ambulance and told dispatch there was no hurry; she was dead. The elbows of her thin denim jacket had worn through; so had her skin. X-rays of her elbows and forearms would later show that she must have crawled the last few hundred feet on exposed bone. Ironically, the anaesthetic effects of a body full of drugs had kept her pain-free; no one could explain where the strength came from.

Father Etienne LeClerc, a semi-retired priest, administered last rites to dying natives at St. Boniface Hospital; there were never enough First Nations elders to assist with the passage of their own, a sad fact, but he didn't mind pitch-hitting. Father Etienne was seventy-two, old enough to have known people who remembered the Métis rebellions led by Louis Riel; he'd ministered to survivors of the Canadian government residential schools where native children, forcibly removed from their families, were beaten for speaking, even during sleep, in their cradle tongues. The white man's God—his God—was going to have some 'splaining to do; meanwhile, there was a DOA just out of Triage—aboriginal female; estimated age, twelve; no ID, evidence of spontaneous abortion; fetus, unaccounted for.

He approached a gurney in the refrigerated ward where the deceased were held until instructions for the disposal of remains were given. According to the chart, the body underneath the sheet weighed seventy-two pounds; in length—one could not ascribe height to a being so curled, so folded in on herself—was five foot, seven inches.

Father Etienne folded the sheet back lengthwise. Nuns had removed her street clothing; it lay, reeking of filth and dried blood, in an open cardboard box beside her, and they'd dressed her in a white cotton hospital gown patterned with tiny violets. The gown was thin but clean and neatly pressed; he liked that.

The dead, the old priest believed, had things to say and the right to say them before he turned them over to the Higher Authority; and those who'd lived and died on the streets, as this poor child had, had nothing but their bodies as final testimony. And so, from an internal distance that allowed him to take note, should they occur, of his own fears and revulsions, he proceeded to acquaint himself with his newest charge.

To his surprise, the girl's arms and lower legs were thickly bandaged; someone in triage must have held out hope, despite the Dead On Arrival sign-off. It was a false hope; she had no body fat, no reserves. Her twiggy brown thighs were pock-marked killing fields, scarred purple and black from beatings and bad needles.

Her face was small and round with a pointy chin; the shape reminded him of a rose leaf. Her thin brittle hair turned rusty bore the signs of malnutrition and long-term drug abuse, but one didn't notice so much these details because of that face to which he was drawn again. She had the fawn-shaded skin of pure blood Swampy Cree; her cheeks were surprisingly full, and her plum-coloured lips formed a perfect bow. He could imagine how she might have looked when her nation's people walked proud and free, before the pelt-hungry Hudson's Bay Company lured them into trapping for liquor and cheap tinware.

The finest warriors would have come for miles around, competing in games of prowess for her hand. He imagined how her long-lashed eyes—closed now, of course—would look when luminous with hope and good humour. They would be dark brown, he surmised, with a deep mauve cast of wild roses at twilight.

The priest turned away from her to unfold the canvas camp stool that served as portable altar, and on this he placed the satchel that contained holy water, a crucifix and other last rite supplies. While thus engaged, entertaining still his fantasy of a strong beautiful Cree woman living a life free of brutality, he caught peripheral movement from the bed.

Post-mortem contractions and twitches were common enough, but that wasn't what he'd seen or felt. This had registered more as a brushing movement, like the sweep of a shawl intended to catch his attention.

He crossed himself and said, "Hello, I'm Father Etienne. Was there something you wanted to tell me?"

Her eyelids squeezed briefly.

"Holy Mother in Heaven." He took her cold, wafer thin hand in his. "Have you decided to return to us?"

A roaring emotion surged upward from the pit of his belly, a massive force like the inrush of sea through a breaking levee. The stimulus, the power of it, made him feel fifty years younger; he could have leaped to his feet right then and clicked his heels. But none of these sensations were registering on the girl, apart from the continued tightening of her eyelids, which had been relaxed moments ago, had they not?

Etienne was certified by St. John's Ambulance to administer first aid, and so his hands began the motions of searching for a pulse and other signs of life, while his mind chased down the image of his friend, bush pilot Ed O'Neill, who delivered groceries, fuel and donations to the 750 Swampy Cree of Innis Landing every week. The priest accompanied him several times a year to perform weddings, baptisms and other sacraments.

He checked his watch; Ed was scheduled to fly from Winnipeg Airport in less than two hours. "Wait here," he said, to the prone and battered body. "If you want to live, live. If burial on the shores of Hudson Bay among your own nation is why you've flooded me with this sudden youthful recklessness, then you'll have to pardon me. I have phone calls to make."

By day's end, Father Etienne had pulled enough strings and called in enough favours to deliver Elsie Kalahash to Innis Landing, where Jimmy Small Beaver mistook her for a sleeping bag. With the error sorted, he carried her in the dignified, wordless manner of a Swampy

Cree warrior to the cabin of Bertha Spotted Turtle, healer and chief elder, who recognized in the comatose young woman the Medicine Wheel apprentice she'd been awaiting for years. Three months before dying peacefully in his sleep at the age of eighty, Father Etienne took one last flight to Innis Landing, where he was given the elder's seat of honour at the North position of the wheel, to witness Elsie receiving her Maškēkowak medicine name, Stalking Rose.

By midnight, the party we hadn't planned at the cabin that wasn't ours on Hayden Lake was rocking. The plastic battery wall clock in the kitchenette ticked off seconds, minutes and hours, as usual, while guests of fame and literary merit kept pouring in from larger measurements of time. Sometimes they arrived at the door, other times through chinks in the log walls. A Sumerian whose name I would never remember, who wrote the first recorded acrostic poem on wet clay 4300 years ago, dropped from a strip of fly paper hanging above the coffee table, spilling Pablo Neruda's pisco sour across a complicated poem that Ginny and Herman Melville were co-writing, their arms around each other's shoulders, singing whaling songs like a pair of drunked tars. Later, I would ask Ginny, who imbibed only ginger ale that evening, where she had learned whaling songs, and she answered, "I didn't. The words were just there, like the inside of my head had become a teleprompter."

One of the Irish poets—Yeats, I think—sopped up the mess and brought Saggil-Kinam-I-forget-the-rest to the cooler on the counter that contained an inexhaustible supply of everyone's favourite beverages. I don't know who brought the cooler, but from it Yeats pulled a cork-stoppered clay flagon, and the Sumerian exclaimed in a guttural parlance that somehow translated at my end as, "Hot-diggety dog, warm barley beer!"

I'd never seen my Ginny so luminous. Those gold sparks I'd seen flying off her earlier surrounded her now, hovering steadily like an atmosphere of her own—I'm going to make up a word here—planetude. I wondered if we were all constructed that way, as walking and magnetic centers that pulled . . . pulled what, I didn't know. In

Ginny's case, there was no doubt; she was attracting precisely what she loved most. Every new arrival, she hugged and greeted like a long lost friend, and the affection was mutual. She always made sure I was included in her enthusiasms, either by dragging the new guest to me or vice versa, but after about the fourth embarrassing, "Alain, I'm sure this gentleman needs no introduction," I had to pull her aside and tell her, "I'm sure John Donne's elegies would knock my socks off, but I've never read him. I'm no poet, Sugarbean, and I have no clue what these guys look like in the flesh. And don't you think this is all just a bit creepy?"

"No, why should I? This is fabulous. It's just the kind of Original Unity of the First Thing event Poe foresaw as normal."

Because I hadn't read *Eureka* either, I had no intelligent comeback. Apart from the slight wobble of the cabin's physical dimensions, and the fact that the guests who seemed to number twenty seemed equally, when I tried to count them, to extend like computer-generated crowds to infinity, the ones nearest us were as flesh and blood solid as Ginny and me.

"But what about that wig pomade of Casanova's?" I said, determined to restore some element of cynicism. "Did you smell it? Geez, that would resurrect the dead."

"Now you're just being crude, Alain. I have to get back to our guests. Giacomo is staring."

"So now you're on a first name basis."

"Peppercorn, shut up."

Giacomo Casanova, the world's greatest lover. Yes, he popped in from the woodwork too, wearing a puffed sleeve shirt unlaced at the chest and emerald green breeches, to a loud and welcoming chorus of, "Caa-saa-noo-vaaa!" To my surprise, he was scrawny and pigeon-chested with bad skin, the prototype of a twentieth-century rock star. Someone handed him a tulip of champagne, which he accepted with a bow and extended pinky, and then he twirled on one buckled shoe and exclaimed, "But where are all the women?"

With a heroic leap, I positioned myself adroitly between him and Ginny and held up my beer in male solidarity. "I've been wondering that myself, dude."

He looked at my posture, the exaggerated flexing of my biceps and laughed, a sound that was manlier than his godawful perfume, I can tell you. He stood on tiptoe and caught sight of my gal in the company of Patricia (PK) Page and Enheduanna, the red-haired Babylonian high priestess-poet, and cried, "Ah, there they are!"

I lunged to tackle him. Hayden Brougham, original owner of the cabin, grabbed my sleeve and yanked, clearing the space for Casanove to glide toward our gaggle of gals. "Let him be, he's a good guy. You've got nothing to worry about."

"But why is he here?"

"He's one of the P's, obviously."

"What?"

"On the invitation. Didn't you read it?"

"There was no invitation. You guys just showed up."

"It's probably still in the letter box."

I wanted to stay where I could see the Venetian seducer chatting up the ladies. Maybe I was hoping to pick up a few tips, but Hayden had piqued my interest too. After assuring myself that Giacomo wasn't going to spike Ginny's drink with some eighteenth-century love drug, and that her response to him wasn't more heartfelt than what she had displayed toward Blake, Nietzsche or Keats—but wait, something was wrong. Something different had crept into her eyes. She had risen from the sofa to greet Casanova; she'd stepped away from the coffee table that had become the nexus of a circle of creativity with writers taking notes and reciting, while sharpening quills and 2B graphite pencils.

Hayden's elbow jabbed my ribs. "Let's go check that letterbox, buddy. The lake view this time of night, you don't want to miss it."

"Yeah, okay."

He nudged our way outside and sure enough, in the wooden letter box beside the door, there was a vellum envelope addressed to Mistress V. Coulthard and Mister A. C. Dexter in elegant copperplate, sealed with a blob of red wax. "When did this get here?"

"Questions that begin with when, have no place here." Hayden peered over my shoulder. "Yep, that's it, all right." He settled into one of two cane-back chairs, fished a pipe and tobacco from his pocket and proceeded to fix himself a smoke.

The ground-level plank porch with a balustered cedar railing extended the full width of the cabin. Hayden's chair faced the lake; the other, at a ninety degree angle from his, afforded a view into the cabin through the window where Ginny, not so long ago, had been working on her thesis on *Eureka*. That's when it hit me. She was missing Poe!

I sat down and broke the seal of the envelope. Inside was a single square of heavy stock rag.

> *You are cordially invited*
> *to a Circularity of Glosas*
> *at the domicile of H. A. Brougham,*
> *Hayden Lake, three leagues*
> *upstream from Valletta Falls.*
> *BYOP or P or P*
> *This is an equal opportunity party.*

I turned the card over; there was nothing on the back. "Who sent this?"

The tobacco in Hayden's pipe glowed an orange-red beacon while he sucked. "Abréu calls him The Host."

"Are you sure it's a he?"

"Nope." He stared out across the shimmering oval of hematite that wouldn't have borne his name in the days he lived here. The moon, at the moment, was hidden behind a dense fringed curtain of cedar and tall pines, but the night sky above the clear, still lake exploded with stars. In the water's reflection, I could pick out constellations—the Pleiades, Orion, and most spectacular of all was the Milky Way, our galaxy; it splashed across the heavens like a lactating Universal Breast.

Hayden's eyes narrowed through the aromatic vapors that swirled into braids, rose and drifted off. "You're not one of those suffragettes, are you?"

"Me? No." From my vantage with the lake to my left, Hayden and the cabin window to my right, I was able to see the milling guests inside to about neck level. A heavily veined, liver-spotted hand emerging from a conservative tweed suit was perusing the pages of Ginny's research. I watched her hand pointing something out—a conversation of fingertips—and I recognized in that teleprompter way Jorge Luis

Borges, the brilliant Argentine writer who viewed life as labyrinth and mirrors. Hot dang! I hoped that Ginny would remember all the conversations she was having to recount them to me later.

Hayden was, apparently, waiting for me to elaborate on the subject of suffragettes.

"Women got the vote nearly a century ago," I said. "So have people of colour. Most of the social movements of your era had run their course by the time I could spell my name. Political correctness is our new demon oppressor."

"Oh, yeah? Sounds boring." He propped his heels on the railing and sat back.

"You have no idea."

One of the few things I'd pieced together about the gathering was that time discrepancies didn't seem to bother anyone. Take Hayden, for example: a bronze plaque in the Brougham College Rare Editions Library marked his life span as 1893-1917, and he carried the perceptions and prejudices of his time, and yet he didn't waste intelligence or this opportunity wondering how I could be from 1995, seventy-eight years distant, in the same way that one wouldn't say to a party guest in Prague, "What do you mean, you came from Cincinnati?"

I examined the invitation again and wondered if it had been in the letterbox when Ginny and I arrived, what, a day ago. "So what do you know about this Host?"

"Not much. He's not without his wit. BYOP or P or P, have you figured that out yet?"

I took a long swig of Heineken, noting, as an aside, that my present level of mild inebriation didn't fluctuate; and come to think of it, the 12-pack that should have been drunk dry hours ago, had been three-quarters full when I helped myself to this one. "Well, based on the guest line-up, I'd say Bring Your Own Poetry . . . or Prose . . ." I thought of Nietzsche and Epictetus. "or Philosophy?"

"Three for three, well done." He reached out and high-fived me. "Every party mix is based on the preferences of the physical end points—in this instance, the end points are you and your girlfriend.

You're both writers, I gather, although from what I've observed, she's more . . ."

Imagining the countless ways I believed Ginny to be superior, which I construed to be an expression of my devotion, I felt an intense wave of nausea.

". . . academic," he said.

The envy passed. "She is."

"End points vary, according to propensity. Those with a passion for art, music, or economics would assemble a different Third Place gathering."

"Economists have these gigs?" In my world of 1995, we were deep into corporate acquisitions and mergers, creating the icon of the soulless suit.

"Sure, why not? Each of us is a myriad of intelligences, not a single being at all, connected to and bubbling from infinite other myriads. These celebrations, these—" He leaned over to read the invitation. "What did the Host call this one? Circularity of glosas—ha, I like that—they resonate and challenge to an optimal degree everyone who's shown up. In your normal state of consciousness—which, let me tell you, is going to feel like no hangover you've ever imagined—you might remember this evening as a burst of creativity that popped up from nowhere. Of course, everything pops from somewhere."

"So I won't remember this tomorrow, you and me talking? The way the lake looks?"

"You might. I used to remember . . ."

I caught a look of pain before he turned his head.

Ginny was now seated at her writing table, at the window near Hayden. She was writing longhand in the black Moleskine journal I'd given her for her birthday, the one she never wanted to write in, convinced her efforts would be crap. She paused now and again to converse, accompanied by lively hand gestures—who knew hands could convey so much?—with whomever was sitting across from her. And there was that green-horned puke-meister of jealousy again.

What Hayden was describing sounded like the things Ginny quoted from *Eureka.* I wondered why I'd listened so rarely, cutting her off with remarks like, "Would you mind, Gin? I'm deep into Arthur C. here."

My career as a best-selling author was mapped out in rough, but I hadn't yet settled on a genre.

"So what about this circularity of glosas?" I asked. "I talked to the poet PK Page, she signed her book, and I get that glosas are a form of medieval Spanish poetry, but I don't recall her using the term circularity."

"It was new to me too," Hayden said, "until Abréu explained it. He's half Maltese Jew, you know. His mother's squaw—"

"Whoa, we don't use that term where I come from."

"What, Maltese?"

"No, squaw. And I'd appreciate if you didn't use it."

Hayden gave me a slow, fiendish grin. "Now that wouldn't be some of that—what did you call it—po-li-ti-cal coh-wreck-nness you mentioned earlier?"

I felt the blast-furnace heat of embarrassment. "No, I mean—well, maybe, yeah . . ."

"Squaw, my friend, is Algonquian for woman, a word that's every bit as respectful as *mujer* or *femme*. I was going to say that Abreu's mother was a squaw of the Cree nation. Are you allowed to say Jewess, by the way?"

"Unless you are one, it's not encouraged."

"Okay, I'll keep that in mind. Anyway, Abréu's life thread, that's what we call your origins while you're in the Third Place, is seventeenth century. His father was banished from Jewish society for associating with Shabtai Tzvi, a Kabbalist who cracked and thought he was the One, the Messiah. Tzvi was smuggled to Albania to avoid stoning, while Abréu the Elder was press-ganged by the French government to Canada as a translator and Indian agent. Abréu Junior grew up fluent in Cree, French, English, Spanish, Portuguese and Ladino, the language of Sephardic Jews that's related to Spanish.

"You'd never know to look at him, but he writes poetry in all those languages too. Smart son of a bitch. Some say he's Coyote, a backward-facing Medicine Man. I wouldn't know about that, he's always been straight-up with me. I'd even quit the drugs if I thought I stood half a chance of finding his kind of peace. Anyhow, you asked about glosas.

"Back in medieval European courts, we're talking way back—the 1100s, Eleanor of Aquitaine, if you were ambitious but neither talented nor royal enough to sleep in a feather bed, your prime goal in life would be to become a courtier, to live inside the castle walls, not outside. Once there, though, you were doomed to boredom, standing around whispering intrigues, any one of which could backfire and land you in the dungeon or worse; waiting and hoping for a glimpse of the resident royals, which allowed you, at least, the brief calishtenic of a curtsy or bow. Then, alas, more standing around.

"To alleviate this insufferable condition, troubadours and jesters collaborated to devise form poetry that invigorated sagging court spirits. Abréu's father who was secular enough in his pre-Tzvi days to mingle in the courts remembered, in particular, the mystical power of glosas."

I sat forward in my chair, elbows on knees.

"Imagine the possibility," Hayden continued, "of peeling back the brain or creative center of your favourite writer through four lines of his or her work. Imagine that in the peeling back, you'd find swirling pathways, illuminated filaments of emotion, stories, novels and poetry at their source point of creation, and even better, this discovery feels erotic, like that pre-coital throb that feels almost better than the act itself, if you'll pardon my Latin."

Hayden tapped the ashes of his smoked pipe onto the porch floor. I noticed his hands were shaking, and I had the sudden sense of understanding why his life thread, as he called it, unraveled the way it did.

"To write or hear a glosa every day could give you a high like the jimweed, hypnotize and soothe like the red poppy juice. The writers of glosas could ignite an entire court, elevate their thoughts, their intelligence, their potential and wit." He patted his pockets for a book of matches and brought out the tobacco again. "At the height of the Court of Love, thousands of troubadours were singing and screwing their way from Lisbon to Limoges, but only a few composed circularities of glosas that were so inspiring to courts ravaged by invasion and brutality, that they were granted access to the most privileged inner sanctum available to mankind."

"Like what?" I said. "The king's treasury? Queen's bed?"

"Hell, no!" Hayden sat up and planted both feet on the floor, abandoning the rekindle of his pipe. "Lay not your treasures where they will rust and corrupt. I'm talking about here, where you and I, man, are hobnobbing with the most illustrious minds our species has created. They were granted access to the Third Place."

CHAPTER 4
THE EIGHTEENTH GLOSA

Ginny and I made love while the crescent moon touched the horizon for the last time that night, sunk in a crazy tangle of bed sheets on the oversprung bed that flung us off, laughing and sweaty to the floor where we carried on, rolling, one over the other, palms and soles slapping the hardwood with every heaving thrust of energy we took and gave away.

"Promise me," Ginny cried, at the edge of her final crest while her slender body arced, tensile and quivering, "to never, ever let this. . ." Her nails pulled tattoos of crimson down my back. ". . . night go to waste." Then she howled and I poured into her, a violent exuberance, a joyful exchange of flesh for spirit to oblivion, to flesh again.

We dozed off in each other's arms, sodden and spent, on the braided rag rug, and while I drifted with Ginny spooned in my arms, the wind picked up and the windowpanes rattled and a raven took up its doleful cawing from the top of a nearby jack pine. I sensed someone approaching from across the room behind me, heard it kneel at my back with the pops and cracks of someone slightly out of shape; I heard these details but I wasn't quite awake and I couldn't move. Then came the pressure of a chin against my neck, nose in my hair, just behind the right temple; wet lips touched my ear, breath buzzing against the cartilege and smelling faintly of decay.

"In dark pre-dawn," the voice whispered, "I heard you creeping in."

The raven cawed again.

Bodies of water, like bodies of people, live up to their names. The Tourbillon River, pronounced Turby-on by the English garrison dwellers who received the goods of the French *voyageur* trappers, lived in terror of the shifting eddies and immeasurable depths that swallowed eighteen-foot canoes and small fortunes in timber, never to be seen again.

That the turbulence should source from as benign a lake as Hayden, called the Marriage Bed of Twisted Hair in the oral traditions of Huron and Cree, plunge abruptly at Valletta Falls—Windigo's Jaw in the old tongue—and conclude as picturesque shallow rapids at Mer de Rose where it drained into Lake Superior, was the stuff of legend.

South of the Falls, Elsie and Jenah-Rae walked alongside the Tourbillon. Sometimes their trail hugged the riverbank, while other times, steep outcrops forced them further into the woods, where they picked their way through sphagnum-coated deadwood, fern beds spongy with rain, and tangles of poison oak, cockleburrs and briar. The deepening silence of four-leggeds and the winged nations told Elsie that she and Jenah-Rae were on the right path. In white man's time, they'd been walking forty-four minutes. Had they taken the road directly to the eddy where Alain C. Dexter posted his last Facebook Note, they'd have arrived in under twenty; but all they'd have been able to do is stare thirty meters down an unbreachable cliff, to a watery vortex almost as deep again as the drop.

The tumbling water at the base of Valletta Falls sent its drumlike rhythms outward through the woods to a radius of at least eighty paces, and within that circle, Elsie gave herself over with measured intensity to Stalking Rose, her Swampy Cree medicine woman nature. The falls was singing to her that the *wasichu* had not arrived, which meant that he was still upstream somewhere, and that she and Little Mynx would have to climb an escarpment to higher ground, to reach the turbulent waters.

During her years of apprenticeship with Bertha Spotted Turtle, Elsie had walked hundreds of miles over rocky ground to learn the many dialects of stone. Every aspect of Mother Earth relates to the two-leggeds differently, and few *wasichu* knew this. Every patch of ground has its own temperament, and the granite outcrops on the western bank of the Valletta Gorge had never been welcoming. Hikers who'd attempted to scale these rock walls, which by slope and elevation appeared to be of moderate difficulty, nearly always turned back, if they hadn't already broken bones or been traumatized, unable to climb or ascend.

Stalking Rose carried basic emergency supplies in her light nylon backpack—a forty-foot length of rope, space blankets—but no climbing equipment. The soles of her moccasins were brushed hide so that her toes could grip embedded roots and curl into indentations too shallow for hiking boots. At the sheerest spots, she merely rested the length of herself, one unhurried posture at a time, along the vertical rock, moving when the rock sensed her balance and allowed her to proceed. Stone, like all matter, contains gravitational pull, its own sovereignty, along with the power to reverse it. Medicine men and women with a certain kind of training could see, years after the event, the locations where climbers with axes and spikes didn't merely fall, they were pushed by the rock itself, in retaliation for the invasion of its flesh.

Little Mynx, still early in her apprenticeship, was obliged to take a longer route to the Tourbillon; her synthetic brand-name running shoes would be worse than greased skis on the escarpment, and learning to gauge the gravities and temperament of stone would take her many years. She would meet up with Elsie at the base of the only safe descent on the western wall of the Gorge.

Stalking Rose ascended the escarpment without incident and now stood forty meters above the upper flow of the Tourbillon, with a clear view of the river. Whether Alain Dexter knew that he'd photographed his bare feet three meters upstream from the river's deepest eddy, Elsie didn't know. The vortex was deceptive, at the best of times. Depending on the season and time of day, its great looping spirals could be camouflaged by surface current, and the swift disappearance of people sucked into its depths wreaked havoc on OPP search and rescue efforts. As Bertha Spotted Turtle liked to say, gone is gone.

A single rivulet, lined with gravel that was polished to ball bearings, allowed passage from the summit of the west flank to the river's edge. Stalking Rose stepped into the shallow, biting cold water and arms out for balance, allowed herself to roll down like a suitcase down a luggage chute.

She continued about forty paces along the base of the gorge at the river's edge until she came to something that filled her with a peculiar mixture of excitement and dread. A great Eastern cedar, a grandfather tree, had toppled across the Tourbillon from east to west. Its highest needles came nearly to her toes. His massive root system, torn from the cliff wall across the river, stood at least two stories high. He must have lost his grip during spring melt.

Shocked and saddened, Stalking Rose lay her hands along a top bough. "My heart weeps, Grandfather, to see that you have fallen, and my heart sings at the great life you have lived, sheltering and nourishing the beings of Mother Earth."

She recalled something that Bertha Spotted Turtle had said to her: "Trees watch the people who pass by them. They only need to see a two-legged once, and that memory is eternal. When a single tree falls, its stories are held by the Tree nation for safekeeping." Stalking Rose had walked these woods and this river bed hundreds of times with her teacher; on her own, she slept in these woods in solitary retreat, developing the endurance and the skills required of the Backward-Facing Path. The Grandfather cedar had been a reassuring presence as he clung to the eroding gorge wall, defying storms and gravity to reach his full height. And as she formed these thoughts, she felt in the marrow of her bones an oscillating, blue-green profundo bass that formed the words: *You are aligned in most of the stories you tell yourself, apprentice to Spotted Turtle,*

In most?

The tree had not addressed Stalking Rose by her medicine name, which confirmed that she heard the message truly. In the gradations of Medicine Wheel, balance and respect underscored all things, and tradition maintained that she would be addressed by all aspects of Great Spirit as "apprentice to Spotted Turtle", her teacher, until the training of her own apprentice Little Mynx was complete, or until she was awarded a male counterpart, her equal in medicine skills and prowess.

"Your acknowledgment honours me, Grandfather, and I would be grateful to learn which of the stories I carry are not in alignment with Manitou, Great Spirit."

The tree did not answer through words, or through vibrations that the human energy body translates into words. Instead, he guided her attention to inspect the length of him, to travel her gaze through layered filigrees of branch and bough, through flat-leafed needle sprays, some green but most rusted with age to a crimson flapping movement near the roots.

Our falls were timed, Grandfather said. *I have been letting go my roots for years, but he is only beginning. You will assist him in his release. You will train him in the turnings of the Medicine Wheel, and in so doing, gain recognition of your name.*

Shock and protest erupted from Stalking Rose's bones, heart and bloodstream, as she comprehended the significance of the dangling mass in red plaid at the far end of the tree, whose life force spluttered and snapped like downed electrical wires.

"*Wasichu,*" she spat, loudly enough that the snakes who lay dozing under river stones woke and lifted their heads. White man!

Jenah-Rae, at that moment, surfed down the rivulet like the snowboarder she was, to the water's edge and bounded the forty paces to Elsie, exclaiming: "You've found him!"

⁕

I pulled the quilted comforter off the bed and covered Ginny, who lay sleeping, curled and naked on the rug, where we'd made love and promises, and I went to the bathroom.

Echoes of laughter and conversation from the party rang through my head like background music where I could pick up the lyrics—*one small kiss to win her spirit*—and sing along if I wanted to allow the phrasing to play on. As if it would always be there.

Our BYOP, P or P circularity bash had broken up around three a.m., clock time. I had already dismissed the apparition who'd disturbed my sleeping-awake state by muttering into my right ear. I didn't even want to dignify the visitor by calling it an apparition. Apparitions appear—they block your path. It's the confrontation that startles, and if the apparition *appears* larger, stronger, meaner, smarter, fear sets in. Otherwise, big deal.

I flushed the toilet and pulled on a pair of sweat pants that I'd thrown over the shower rod yesterday. Funny that Ginny had never yanked them down when the guests started arriving.

Instead of returning to bed—it was still dark, and a couple hours more shut-eye would have been nice—I went to the writing table near the window where, in the midst of Ginny's research chaos, her Moleskine journal lay open. The left page had been weighted with a fist-sized rose quartz and granite rock, the kind that lined our beach, the kind that Ginny would keep as a souvenir of our holiday.

On the weighted page, the number 18 had been written, followed by four lines of poetry scribed in a heavy hand with old-fashioned loops and whorls. Below and to the right of the quatrain, as in an epigraph was written: *"The Coliseum", Edgar Allan Poe*. The rest of the page and the one across it were blank—had been left blank, was the feeling I got.

Something immediate shot through me. I recalled someone—had it been Abréu?—mentioning that Poe had been detained at the Coliseum, and in my strange, neither-here-nor-there state, it made perfect sense that Ginny's beloved Edgar Allan would drop by, better late than never, and leave these tantalizing lines for Ginny.

Not for Ginny.

I looked around. "What?"

Notforginnynotforginnynotforginny—too-wheet!

Oh. It was a bird. One of those cheepy little sparrow wren types, small, brown, drab, I could never tell them apart, was sitting on the cedar rail of the porch, staring at me with bright little eyes.

If not for Ginny, then for whom? I read Poe's quatrain . . .

Not all our power is gone—not all our fame—
Not all the magic of our high renown—
Not all the wonder that encircles us—
Not all the mysteries that in us lie—

. . . and without thinking, picked up a pen and drew a few asterisks to set off his lines, then wrote the words that had been whispered to me after Ginny and I made love. *In the pre-dawn dark, I heard you creeping in.* It was as good an opening line as any.

Humming to myself in a kind of manic trance, I composed four, ten-line stanzas, each of which ended, successively, with one of Poe's lines. In addition to our corresponding themes, his work and mine blended with the rhymed end words in lines six and nine that presaged his line ten. In less than half an hour, I had written a perfect draft of my first, and as things would transpire, my only glosa. I set down the pen and went to have a shower.

A short while later, beard trimmed and smelling of Irish Mist, I emerged from the foggy bathroom to the aromas of fresh brewed coffee and cinnamon toast. Outside, the wind had died down, and a thick fog had descended; it pressed against the windows and looked bubbly and lumpy, like a lobster bisque on low simmer. I felt happy to see Ginny, seated at her table with a mug of coffee, the Moleskine open in front of her, but instead of finding her beaming with astonishment or loving admiration, she looked pissed.

"You bastard," she said. "How could you do this to me?"

"—the hell?" I snugged the bath towel around my waist. "I know it's only my first attempt, Sugarbean, but, geez—"

"Don't you call me that! I don't ever want to hear that word coming from your mouth again. And what do you mean, it's your first attempt? You plan on making a career of this, or something?"

"Writing glosas?" My snort of laughter shot out a booger, and I discovered, heading toward the coffee pot, that wiping away snot is a lot gentler on a guy's dignity than the effort of trying to understand a woman. "I don't think even Patricia entertains those kinds of ambitions."

"Patricia, which one's she? The banged or the neglected one?"

"Huh?"

"Fine, play stupid or glib, whatever you think you're doing, but my dream wedding in Fiji, that is too much. I thought I knew you, Alain. I can't believe you'd use my beautiful journal for your sick fantasies—"

"Hold on, right there. For one thing, I gave you that journal. Wanna check the inscription? Secondly, I thought you'd be pleased, Poe and I surprising you. You knew he was held up at the Coliseum, right?"

She tipped her head and looked at me as if I'd poured coffee down my pants.

I helped myself to a piece of cinnamon toast and stayed behind the kitchenette counter where I figured it was safer to eat my stand-up breakfast.

"There was this moment at the party last night," I said, "where you looked so sad. I thought it was because of him . . . I mean, there we all were—Blake, Milton, Dickens, even a couple of Sumerians, for chrissake!—living proof of *Eureka*, his theme of space and duration being one. We really do endure, at least, the greatest of us do." I chewed and stared through the kitchen window at nothingness. "I may not have captured that internal beyondness in my glosa. I would have liked to name the Third Place outright, but I'm not sure we're allowed, and it probably wouldn't have fit in the rhyme scheme." I blinked and zoomed out from wherever I'd been musing and glanced around. "When did you clean up? You should have waited. I would have helped."

"Clean up what?"

"The bottles, the coolers, the food. Did you try that otter jerky Abréu brought? I didn't know what it was, otherwise I'd have never . . . Ginny, why are you looking at me that way?"

"We didn't have people over last night. You fell asleep at 7:30, snoring with Azimov on your chest. And I don't appreciate your mockery of Poe and my dissertation topic."

A cocktail of stress hormones were pumping through my system. I looked at the coffee table, hub of last night's genius, and there were the fishing magazines, neatly fanned, and Ginny's pen, lying exactly the way it had landed when she threw it yesterday.

But I knew what I knew and saw what I saw.

"I'm not mocking anything," I said. "We both heard the knock on the door. You're the one who told Abréu and Hayden they could come in. I thought you were crazy."

Ginny dropped her head into her hands. I was certain that when she looked up, she'd have remembered, or she would admit that she was messing with my head in a nasty way.

"Okay, we need to leave now," she said. "If we don't return the car before noon, we'll get charged for another day. I've already packed my clothes, I just need to gather these notes."

I finished my coffee and crossed the room. "Why are you pushing away the most extraordinary event of our lives? You said it yourself while we were making love. 'We must never, ever forget this night.' And what's this crap about leaving? We have another six days."

I claimed the chair across from her, for once, free of notebooks. What more proof did she need that I was occupying the very spot where John Donne and Alfred, Lord Tennyson had taken gentlemanly turns writing, laughing, enjoying her company the way I used to, and longed to again.

Her eyes were tearing; the anger dissolving into something that resembled pity. "Alain, please . . ."

"Here, look at this." I picked up the Moleskine and riffled through the pages. "I understand why you'd be flatlining this morning—I mean, who in their right mind could believe it? But here's your proof, glosa after glosa, composed in the presence of the masters themselves. I'm your eye witness, babe—the only one you got."

I riffled through the front half of the journal a second and third time, but she refused to look. She seemed to have settled into some kind of catatonia. I examined the pages and sure enough, they were filled with glosas in rough draft, borrowing quatrains or four lines of prose from history's greatest writers. She had even numbered them, there were seventeen—only they were all written in Ginny's hand.

Still, I was not going to let something so trivial get in the way. "You wrote these last night in collaboration, I watched you. Over there at the coffee table, which was a whole lot messier at 2 a.m., you and Herman Melville sang whaling songs while you co-penned your glosa, 'Reviving the Blue Balloon.' I admit, I was a little worried when Casanova arrived that he would seduce you and you'd run off with him to Venice, and the male/female ratio was hard to take at first. That's partly why Hayden and I spent so much time on the porch."

"Alain," Ginny said in a voice that sounded 10,000 miles distant. "Today is the tenth of May, it's our last day of vacation. These glosas you think I wrote last night, I've been working on all week. They gave me a head break from the thesis."

Something was slipping away from us, drifting into the fog like an unmoored canoe. If what she was saying was true, that eight days had passed and our vacation was over, I would deal with it. Later. Right now, what mattered was restoring Ginny's recall because if there weren't at least two of us who could admit to participating in a Circularity of Glosas—and on this, I would wager my mother's life—something vast and life-giving, something that pulsed at the quantum point of thought/form convergence would become forever irretrievable.

I opened the journal to the eighteenth, the final, glosa. "Look at the handwriting of the quatrain I borrowed to write, um . . ." I had to look again at the title I'd given to my piece. ". . .'Unbreaking Fine Threads'. Does that look anything like my penmanship?"

Ginny chewed on a thumbnail. "No, it doesn't, and you did a pretty good job imitating his signature. Those loopy e's, the pressure of the pen . . ."

"But I didn't write this. It was already written, waiting, held open by a—" I glanced around. "Look, this rock, this very rock was holding the journal open to the excerpt of Poe's 'Coliseum' when I got up after we made love."

Ginny had shimmering gray-blue eyes that could turn like the mid-Atlantic from stormy to calm and back again. Until that moment, however, I had never seen the light drain away.

"You gave me this rock," she said, "on our hike to Valletta Falls five days ago. You called it our engagement stone, a placeholder for the time when your book hits the best-seller list and you can afford to buy me a diamond. You don't remember?"

My heart and lungs felt like they were being squeezed by a red-hot pair of flatirons. I had no memory of what she had just described, and if I had said those things, they felt cheesy. Ginny Coulthard had never struck me as one of those women who would waggle her left hand to girlfriends as if she'd just scored a deal at a slave auction. I was starting to feel sick to my stomach.

And then to my relief, I spotted, buried under papers, the corner of a yellow-ochre, softcover book. I pulled it out. "Here, look at this! *Hologram* by P.K. Page. She asked me to call her Patricia. We're her friends, see? She signed it to both of us."

Ginny and Alain, to you both, I wish long lives of adventurous prose and poetic thrill . . .

—a fellow glosera, PK Page, May, 1995

It was my first time reading the inscription. There'd been so much going on, all the guests arriving. I felt certain this piece of evidence would clinch it.

But the sting of despair on Ginny's face proved the end of the road. I almost knew what she was going to say.

"Ms. Page signed this at her book launch event in the Hayden Library the day before we came here. I asked you to come with me, I thought you'd really like her, but you said you needed to work on your novel outline."

A vice-like pain, some age-old stubbornness, a part of me I hated but had learned to live with, tightened at my temples. I remembered making that excuse; she attended the book launch alone, and I never wrote a word of the outline. I played some video game instead. "I'm sorry, Ginny, that sucks. I wish I had been kinder." *I wish I could be kinder.*

She took the book from me and began to gather her notes. "It doesn't matter. None of this matters. But I need to tell you something, Alain, and you need to listen. If we're going to spend our lives together, I will not tolerate what you describe in this glosa—no way, no shape, no form of it. If something about *Eureka* has persuaded you of a new capacity, some larger reality, that's great. But this—" She pecked hard at the Moleskine with her fingernail. "This is out of bounds, non-negotiable. If you have any doubts on that score, you'd better walk away now." She stood and looked down at me. "Because if you don't, if you go all macho, thinking you can test those boundaries, I will make what remains of your life a living hell."

CHAPTER 5
THE SMOKING

Jenah-Rae Chappell had never attended a smoking before and thought it was so cool, she didn't even mind that they would never make it to their campsite at Pukaskwa. Little Mynx, her adopted Maškēkowak spirit self, who stalked and circled her one-quarter Haida self and the Chinese and Jamaican parts with every diastolic beat of their one heart, knew it didn't matter. Surfing and beach volleyball could wait; the unconscious man lying on a bed of moss wouldn't.

The rescue took them longer than it should have because Jenah-Rae was terrified of heights, and the Tourbillon River, swollen with spring flood, roared beneath their feet, its deepest eddy swirling just downstream. They had to crawl across an enormous fallen Eastern cedar. It had a scratchy trunk and a million tangled branches with dead leaf sprays that crumbled to powder at the touch and flared up her allergies; there'd been a hornet's nest and little red ants that bit and large black ones that tried to crawl into her eyes and ears. About halfway across, Jenah-Rae thought she would go mad from the slapping and sneezing, but then Elsie Stalking Rose, said something sharply to her in Swampy Cree, and everything inside went quiet.

From then on, things flowed. They harnessed the man who'd been snagged by a heavy bough at the back of his jacket; he hung like a scarecrow, arms outstretched, head and hands flopped, his legs submerged to the knees and bouncing in the rapids. Stalking Rose whipped up a net of knots and slings with one of the coils of nylon rope from her backpack, creating two looped handles for each of them to pull the man across the water, using the river's downstream current to buoy him and take most of the weight. There was no way to ascend the eastern wall of the gorge, the side he'd jumped from, so they had to crawl again across the cedar, passing their human cargo hand over hand through all the same obstacles, only they didn't seem so bad the second time.

How they got him up the western flank of Valletta Gorge, Jenah-Rae didn't think she'd ever fully understand. The slippery little brook that got them down was useless in the other direction, and yes, Elsie was a cop with survival training; the knots she tied at the top of the gorge were as sturdy as the ones she'd anchored at various roots and protuberances on the rock wall itself.

"It will take us three stages," she told Jenah-Rae at the riverbank where the man lay nearby, good as drowned if you ignored the old medicine. "First, I get you to the top."

With the inner silence still in place, Jenah had been able to climb the three ropes without too much trouble. At the top, Elsie grabbed her hand, pulled her onto flat ground and gave her shoulder a squeeze. "Well done. Now, you stay here to guard the third rope. I'm going down again. For him."

There was an old song her Mom used to sing before she got too sick, called, "He Ain't Heavy, He's My Brother". Jenah had always thought it was corny, but there were no other words to describe how Elsie Stalking Rose was able to carry a man over six feet tall, outweighing her by at least fifty pounds, strapped to her back. She used the climbing ropes in the ordinary way; she found toeholds and indentations, but there were places on the rock wall where it seemed all she did was rest.

Now they were deep in the woods in a small clearing, and they had a fire going. Jenah, at Elsie's instruction, had gathered a pile of wet grass and green sticks four feet high. Their patient—or what Elsie called "a gift from the mysterious ways of Manitou—lay naked and wrapped in silver space blankets, with only his red-bearded head and bare feet exposed. His red plaid jacket, jeans, T-shirt and boxers lay stretched across juniper and bare rocks to dry. Someday, Jenah-Rae was going to piss herself laughing at how much the man resembled, in his foil wrappings, a giant hot dog. When she looked at his cold gray skin, and the way he didn't breathe, the prospect of laughter prevented her from thinking he was dead.

The driver of the logging truck had not seen our cherry red Honda on the less than two-lane stretch of Hwy. 147, where Ginny had been unable to pull over, and it didn't occur to either of us to turn on the hazards.

The fog was worsened; it was thick as pillows, and the last words I heard from Ginny as she worked through the range of headlights was, "They all shine back at me. I can see better without them."

Last thing I said to her was, "Pull over, I'm gonna hurl."

The impact of the logging truck that was traveling sixty kilometers per hour, legal speed, snowplowed the Civic nearly twenty metres before the shocked driver was able to fully engage his brakes. Ginny died instantly, crushed between glass, metal and upholstery. I don't remember the ambulance taking us to the hospital or the OPP driving me home alone to our dorm apartment. No charges were laid. I vaguely remember the funeral, her family members telling me it was not my fault; the strangeness of their hugs, bending over from the waist, arms like coatracks. *Pat, pat, pat.* I never saw any of the Coulthards again.

For the next seven years, I just kept moving. I'd done some acting in high school and college and took it up again professionally in regional theatres across Canada: I did stints backstage, designing sets, directing, now and again. Perpetually broke and stressed, I gave up the idea of writing novels and penned instead satirical, deeply angry short stories that grew to sufficient quantities to become a collection. *Gizzard's Luck & Other Organic Festivities* won a Governor's General award and was shortlisted for the UK Man Booker prize.

In 2002, the height of my semi-fame, I met and married Carolyn Allbright, a tiny brunette with a sweet smile. An admin assistant for a locksmith company, she attended one of my readings in Toronto, stood in line for two hours for an autograph, and turned five shades of white, pink and red when I asked her out for coffee. Award funds and speaker fees paid, barely, for our splurge wedding-honeymoon in Fiji (my idea) where we walked on a bed of coals as a symbol of trust and to earn good fortune from the Polynesian gods. The *Toronto Star* published a colour photo in their Life section of the quirky Canadian author-actor with his lovely new bride dancing on coals. My book sales rose; business is business.

When we returned to Canada, the South Pacific gods were as good as their word. Brougham College, the alma mater I hadn't set foot on in seven years, offered me the position of House Master for a newly built student residence and a job in Admissions for Carolyn. Not bad for a thirty-one-year-old with a paltry B.A., an overdrawn account, and not a shred of self-respect.

❦

The first thing Elsie Stalking Rose observed about the man lying on the bed of moss, even before she began smoking him, was that he had drowned long before he jumped into the Tourbillon River. She made a small clicking sound with her tongue and turned to Jenah-Rae, who sat crosslegged beside the wet kindling she'd been instructed to collect.

"Little Mynx, do you remember me telling you about the Twisted Hair?"

"Yes, they were storytellers from long ago, traveling women who united the nations from the Andes in the south to the Arctic nations in the far north."

"Indeed. The Twisted Hair, the best of them, were given medicine, a special training, to heal the wounds that cannot be seen. You and I have done many ceremonies with tobacco and pollen, following the ways of the Good Red Road, the road of balance and the physical world. To save this man, I must travel the Blue Road, the non-physical, the road we must all take after death. To do this requires the alignment and protection of the doubled Medicine Wheel. This is the way of Snake, of Coyote, sometimes called the Backward-Facing Path, and it holds many risks.

"This *wasichu* should have died lifetimes ago, and yet Manitou has chosen to spare him and to enlist our aid."

Jenah-Rae's solemn dark eyes never left her.

Stalking Rose continued. "I ask you now to sit firm where you are. On the Medicine Wheel, you occupy the seat of Innocence in the South. You are also keeper of the smoke. Whenever I signal with that clicking sound you just heard, you must add two handfuls of wet kindling to the fire, first with your left hand and then with your right. Do you understand?"

"Left, then right," she said, holding up each hand in succession.

"Exactly. Now this man lies at the East, the Place of Invitation and of Higher Ground. As you can see, I have positioned his head to the North, place of Wisdom, here to my left. His feet are at the South, where you will guard his Innocence with your own.

"I shall be working from two places: West, place of Chaos, and North, across from you. The fire in the center represents our Ancient Heart or the Sacred Zero. To cross the Sacred Zero, to move back and forth over it, is extremely dangerous and must never be attempted without guidance."

Little Mynx nodded, transfixed by Stalking Rose's voice and by the aromatic juniper and cedar that fueled the low crackling fire in front of her. Occasionally, seeds and berries burst, setting off sparks and tiny light shows that would help to keep the girl alert.

"Sometimes you will see me," Stalking Rose continued, "sometimes you won't. When I am not visible, stay calm and remain in your center. I will be walking the ordinal directions of the doubled Wheel and picking up the man's trail.

"If your heart stays open, you may hear his story as he gives it to me. Together, we will gather the broken and dropped threads and twist them whole again. If we succeed, the three of us will walk out of these woods together. If not, then you will take what you observed and bring it to the world. You will share the truth of the Twisted Hair. Are you prepared to do this?"

Jenah-Rae's head bobbed, mouth agape. She was prepared.

"Very well. From here on, we speak only when necessary, in the silent tongue. Keep all of your senses open, Little Mynx. Reject nothing."

Elsie got up from where she had been sitting across from Jenah and moved to the western position of the Wheel, a circular structure about ten feet across with four quadrants that had not been visible to Jenah before, and which she could now trace through faint dots or distortions in the air, like holes punched into an overhead transparency slide.

Stalking Rose, sitting cross-legged, closed her eyes and began to chant. There were no discernible words to the chant, and her lips didn't move; it was more of a rumble that came from deep inside her throat, with variations in sound and pitch controlled by breath and movements of the tongue. It reminded Jenah of videos she had seen of Tibetan monks. She heard a clicking sound—or rather, felt it, like the popping of eardrums in high elevation—and knew it was the signal to throw kindling on the fire. Left hand, then right.

The fire hissed and snapped like an irritated rattlesnake; she thought she saw the flames lunge at her. But she held her place, and the delusion, if that's what it was, receded. Plumes of white smoke rose, dense at first, like thunderclouds, and then thinning out to vertical, wavy threads. Stalking Rose continued to chant, eyes closed, hands open and relaxed in her lap. The pressure in Jenah's ears increased; swallowing didn't relieve it. The air around them hung still, without the slightest breeze; Jenah had registered that. Yet now, while she watched, the smoke, at just below eye level, began to bend. It wasn't blowing toward the man nor dissipating, as smoke will, in an easterly direction; it was bending in response—as Little Mynx explained to her Jenah self— in response to vibratory direction from the base of Stalking Rose's throat.

The smoking of Alain C. Dexter had begun.

By our fifth year of marriage, I had fast-tracked through the Master's and Ph.D. programs at Brougham College. I was now Professor Dexter, Doctor of English Literature, and with the timely aid of attrition and no better candidates (the former estate of Archibald Brougham, though picturesque, is in the middle of nowhere) I became the head of the English faculty.

I created a few fresh ripples in the scholarly realm by writing my dissertation on a little known *voyageur* poet from the seventeenth century fur-trapping era named Abréu de Valletta. He was half Maltese Jew and half Cree, and was something of a local legend. Ghost stories told around campfires often featured Abréu whose spirit was known to shoot off long, slow rounds of musketfire, although no actual acts of violence at his hands had been recorded.

The Hayden Brougham Rare Books Library held the world's only extant folios of his work: 112 poems written in berry dye ink on deerskin and rag parchment, in a chicken-scratch hand and a French-English-Ladino-Cree patois that no one had been able (or bothered) to crack. I cracked it.

My first collection of verse, *Poems from the Soles of His Feet*, was also Abréu's debut in the publishing world. His only reader in the late 1600's had been the Hudson's Bay Company agent at the British garrison near Valletta Falls, site of the now-closed fishing cabin where Hayden Brougham had taken his life in 1917.

Poems from the Soles of His Feet earned moderate acclaim and then envy, enough of both that I began to regard myself as a half-assed poet. In 2008 and 2009, I published two more slim volumes of verse—my own, this time—through Brougham College Press, and because I can throw pizzazz into just about anything, my poetry lectures became the most popular at the school. Even engineers were taking them as electives.

Remember those Polynesian gods? Well, they or someone was still looking out for me. One of my students posted a lecture on ghazals and sestinas on YouTube, and it scored a million views in less than a month. People other than my students began to buy and talk about my poetry on Facebook and in blogs. A Huffington Post reviewer called me the new Robert Bly, which, for reasons I'll go into in a moment, embarrassed me. But in the way of search engines and other small miracles, that comment reached the ear of Bill Moyers who invited me to appear on his new PBS show.

Carolyn, my wife, whom you'll notice, I mention hardly at all, was thrilled. But I wrote an e-mail to Mr. Bly, who is surely one of America's most beloved and authentic poets, right up there with Walt Whitman, and apologized for the comparison. As it happened, he knew of my work and had been the one to recommend me to his friend, Bill. With his characteristic warmth, he advised me to embrace the Muse and never apologize, regardless of what form or forms she took.

Bly being of solid Minnesota Lutheran stock, I'm sure he would not view the habit I'd acquired while still a Teaching Assistant of sleeping with every good-looking female who enjoyed my poems to be "embracing the Muse". Nor being of sturdy English-French lapsed Catholic stock, was my steadfast neglect of Carolyn a worthy example of "never apologize". But I could have swallowed all that and pushed on, continuing to package and re-package my smoke and mirrors talent, if he hadn't ended his message with:

Your work shows traces of the Third Place, which can't be said of many contemporary poets. But do tread carefully, my friend. It is no place for cowards.

Stalking Rose followed the movement of smoke threads from the fire of the Ancient Heart to the East where the red-haired man lay. The Tourbillon River had rejected him; Valletta Falls, if not the eddy, that preceded it, would have spun him quickly to the Good Blue Road. Instead, a Grandfather cedar had chosen that moment to uproot and pull him back.

Alain Dexter's spirit self, summoned by the smoke, manifested not far from the one of flesh and bone. It stood behind his physical, an arm's span further toward the East, wearing an energetic facsimile of the jacket and jeans that lay drying. From where Stalking Rose sat, his spirit and his form appeared perpendicular to one another, like an inverted T.

Smoke threads coiled around the standing figure counterclockwise, slowly, like a cocoon, though not to enclose him. The vapourous filaments kept him visible and in place while Stalking Rose made the necessary adjustments to connect to and inhabit her spirit self. Oral tradition, which predated modern science and was in its way no less scientific, described this operation as building a bridge between the optic nerve and pineal gland in the center of the brain. The latter, also known as seat of the soul or of intuition, had once been walnut-sized, vascular and fleshy in the average human brain; in the twenty-first century, the pineal gland had shrunk to the size and consistency of a dried pea.

A turbulence in her womb area, the pelvic cradle, told Elsie she would soon be invisible to Jenah-Rae, though perhaps not to Little Mynx. A protective disk moved into place at the crown of her head, the fontanelle, to keep her body's life force from escaping in panic. Infants came and went from that spot all the time, while it was soft and pulsing, but then the cranium closed over it to keep us better focused on what lay ahead than above.

The sensations in her pelvic cradle, though intense, stabilized, like an idling motor; the top of her head felt like a bowl-shaped configuration of swarming bees. Her spirit body rose and stood with feet comfortably apart directly opposite the spirit man. She raised her right hand.

"*Wachyia*, hello," she said in silent tongue. "I am Stalking Rose, a Maškēkowak of the Innis Landing Swampy Cree Nation. I am Medicine Woman trained in the Backward-Facing Path."

The spirit man watched and listened. When she had finished, he raised his right hand. "I am Alain Charles Dexter. I have no knowledge of my nation or my roots, not the way you do, but I can see and hear you, and I know that something is keeping me here like a giant thumb, pressed close to this—" He dropped his hand and pointed to the body lying in front of him. "What I don't know is why, or what to do next."

"So it was not your desire to leave the Good Red Road?" she asked.

"Do you mean, did I intend to kill myself? Oh, I did, but from the moment I began tipping forward, I knew that my action would solve nothing. I've tried to reenter the body, and I've tried to leave it. Can't seem to do either. Have I broken some kind of law?"

"Nature's laws cannot be broken. You have been detained, but not as punishment, if that's what you're thinking. If left on your own, your body would eventually decay, but you wouldn't be able to walk on. You'd be caught here as windigo, devouring spirit of the West."

As soon as she named the spirit, she saw an excitation around Alain's physical head, an amorphous sooty movement of many shades of gray. The emotions it exhibited were not unlike a puppy or an infant who knows it has been noticed and wants more, only this had nothing of their sweetness and appeal.

Stalking Rose knew how to hold her reactions, but the size and density of the chaos around Alain exceeded anything that she and Bertha Spotted Turtle had encountered. Even the smoking of an entire Ojibwa village to clean their youth of a glue-sniffing addiction did not compare to what now held this man's cerebral functions hostage.

She sent the signal to Little Mynx to add more kindling. Within moments, the fire hissed and belched and poured out white smoke. This time, the smoke threads wove a loose net around the vicinity of the dark, shifting cloud. Though far from a permanent solution, her intent combined with elemental energy was strong enough to keep the aggressor contained. Knowing the risks, she sidled in a 45 degree angle forward and to her left, bringing her to the Northwest position of the doubled Wheel.

It was like someone had turned up the amplifiers in a torture chamber. She heard shrieks and wails; long vibrato emanations of pain; cruel taunts and laughter; guttering sobs, all the extremities of human anguish compressed into a seething, furious mass that could do nothing but consume itself, excrete and gorge again.

Such was the windigo.

She took an angled step back and to the right, returning her to cardinal West. "What in the name of Manitou have you taken on, Alain Dexter?"

He looked at her sheepishly. "Everything."

Elsie glanced toward Little Mynx who sat firmly stationed in the Innocence at the South; Jenah-Rae's spirit self was not yet capable of full embodiment, but she did send the sensation of a nod. Stalking Rose nodded back. "Very well then."

"You can help me?" Alain said.

"I don't know."

"They said you could."

"Who's they?"

The light of his spirit face flickered and dimmed.

"You can't name names," Stalking Rose said.

He shook his head and opened his hands, palms up. "There are so many of them, and I'm not sure anymore."

Once more, she checked the stability of Little Mynx. Satisfied, she said to Alain, "I'll be moving out of this space and while I'm absent, neither of you will see me. Don't be alarmed, I will come back. It's important for you to stay where you are. No one else can guard your body."

"I can do that," he said.

It's hard to put into words how one travels from one Medicine Wheel station to the next. Imagine a hula hoop and the space inside the tube. The mind intends, energy follows and fills the tube, assuming its shape. At the appropriate station, the energy body rises and reappears. Stories of apparitions and ghosts have alluded to this phenomenon for millennia.

Stalking Rose appeared at the North position and in a single swift motion, too fast to be measured, she and Little Mynx, her young apprentice, created the north-south magnetic poles of a battery. The subliminal light in the forest brightened; birds landed and animals raised their heads, curious to see what was unfolding before them.

The human energy bodies began arriving almost at once, singly and in groups, in dignity and reverence and the quiet hope that are man's true nature.

"My word," Stalking Rose said. "There are a lot of you, and only three of us." If one counted Alain, which she wasn't quite prepared to do.

"We'll see about dat, *ma p'ti rose*," said a familiar, cheerful voice.

From amidst the crowd, two men came into view; one was short and bow-legged and carried a flintlock musket nearly as tall as himself.

"Abréu!" Stalking Rose exclaimed, filling the northern space with firebursts of joy. "I never expected to see you here."

"Why not? These are my stalking grounds."

"Of course, but I heard you'd traveled beyond the Good Blue Road years ago."

"And so I did, then I heard from your teacher that you had 'a situation', so I am here . . . along wit' my friend." He gestured toward a tall, slender man with tawny skin and sharp Mediterranean features. He had chocolate brown eyes and shiny black hair pulled back in a ponytail.

"*Wachyia*, I am Stalking Rose. My heart fills to meet you." As he was a friend of Abréu, she opted for the abbreviated intro.

The man shrugged his shoulders and gave a shy smile of regret.

"This is Gavriel Navarro," Abréu said. "He is a poet and a *voyageur* of the great river to the south, the Amazon. He cannot talk yet. It's his first time in dis place."

"Oh, I see." Stalking Rose remembered her own introduction to a Medicine Wheel smoking. She'd been an apprentice for about eight years with duties that seemed to consist mostly of cleaning Bertha Spotted Turtle's cabin. And then there was a rash of murder-suicides across the Cree communities of Manitoba. Her teacher took her not into the woods, but directly to the realm of pure spirit, and Elsie could not stabilize. The more she tried to manifest, the faster her spirit and physical selves winked in and out of existence. Spotted Turtle's cure was to throw her, naked, into ice-cold Hudson Bay.

"There's no pressure to speak," she assured Gavriel. "You have come to help us, and for that I am glad."

He tipped his head toward Abréu, as if to say, she could speak freely about him and whatever else was on her mind.

She thanked him and used the moment to cast an unhurried gaze at the multitude who had accompanied them. With her expanded vision, she saw that Gavriel was the only spirit body who was currently attached to the physical. In layman's terms, he was the only one who wasn't dead.

"You read correctly," Abréu said. "He is newly famous and our only hope."

"Why do you say that?"

"*Ma p'ti rose*, the time has come and passed and come again to build a bridge between the spirit world and the world of man. A hundred years ago, Hayden Brougham was chosen by Spirit, and we began the work, but he liked the jimweed and the poppy too much, and the bridge collapsed. Seventeen years ago, the man whose body lies now in the East, he and a young woman entered the Tird Place easy as magpies, I thought for sure, we had it in the bag, but no. Something went wrong, and now Monsieur Dexter, he's being eaten alive by the windigo. If we don't free him, if we don't build that bridge between the Good Red

Road and this . . ." He turned and swept his arm in a broad arc to take in the silent, waiting crowd. ". . . the doorway to da Tird Place will be locked forever, and the great mind of Man will be ground like meal for the prairie chickens."

CHAPTER 6
EDGAR ALLAN POE, COME AGAIN

Okay, so where was I? Yeah, here.

Pride goeth before destruction, and an haughty spirit before a fall. So goes the complete verse in the sixteenth chapter of Proverbs, King James edition. The abbreviated finger wag: pride before fall. Abridged or not, I have always taken exception to this verse. Pride in one's work, in one's family, in their achievements, in the health of the community, the nation; pride in the grandeur and beauty of humankind—what is to be dreaded or avoided in these things? I would say instead that shame goes before the fall, guilt and blame its wicked handmaidens. Fall, too, is misleading, so let's rewrite the whole damned thing:

Shame goeth before obliteration, and a collapsed spirit before the rise.

The year was 2010. Carolyn and I had been married eight years, no kids, a mutual non-decision. My growing reputation as a poet-celebrity outside the starving artist borders of Canada still felt like an awkward house guest. We had disposable income; arguments over debt became arguments over how to spend. But here's what I hated most. Carolyn's coworkers in the college admissions office were shunning, their passive-aggressive bullying taking the form of comments like, "I saw your husband on TV last night," or, "Is that another new dress?"

My wife didn't have a gold-digging bone in her body; she bought new clothes because stress-induced dieting shot her weight up and down, and she never felt pretty in anything she wore. We'd long since moved past the stage in our relationship where she'd ask before we went out, "How do I look?" One can only stomach the reply over reading glasses, "Fine", for so long.

I'm giving you this preamble in place of the glowing tribute that Carolyn Allbright Dexter deserved for putting up with an insufferable asshole husband for nearly a decade. Fact is, she deserved better. Second fact, she didn't get it.

The Board of Governors' Awards dinner on September 15, 2010, was the usual demi-glitz affair with dull speeches from people we saw every day and snoozer conversations, over bacon-wrapped filet mignon, about kids' orthodontia and diesel vs. unleaded. Carolyn begged off that night, complaining of a headache. Yes, headaches are a nasty cliché in wedded life, but she had been suffering from them more than usual that summer, so we'd made an appointment with a neurologist in Toronto for mid-October.

So I attended the dinner alone and endured well wishes for Carolyn that, to my guilt-impacted ears, rang sickly-sweet. I drank two carafes of wine between the appetizer and cheese board, and derived scarcely a buzz. At the end of the evening, I bought a bottle of Napoleon brandy from the busty blonde bartender-caterer whose name was Mitzi . . . no, Meredith, at a bootleg price, threw in a $40.00 tip and banged her, with consent, in the back seat of my SUV. When it was over, I reached into a cardboard box I kept for such occasions and handed her an auto-graphed copy of *Gizzard's Luck* from the remaindered stash I bought from the publisher. She may have faked that thrill too.

Every cheating spouse knows that the harder you try to sneak in quietly, the more likely you are to knock over the umbrella stand in the front hall. I stumbled, smelling of sex and Caesar salad, into the kitchen where I microwaved a Pizza Pop, took one bite, burnt the roof of my mouth and threw the rest out.

Something felt off while I climbed the stairs, sliding my hand along the wall, a habit that drove Carolyn crazy. "Do you need me to show you how to use a railing?"

I tripped on a step. Had she just said that? Hissed the words into my right ear, her chin against my neck, nose pressed into my hair? I pushed open the bedroom door, too drunk to wonder why the light was on. Carolyn lay crosswise on the bed in an oversized Tai Chi t-shirt, lower legs hanging over the edge, as if she'd been sitting, adjusting the alarm, and decided to lie back. The circular pool on the white cotton sheets was so large, I thought she was lying on a burgundy satin table-cloth. The aneurysm that killed Carolyn had been growing in her brain for months. She was three days shy of her thirty-eighth birthday.

A medicine woman or man who is trained in the backward-facing path is capable of deconstructing Intent, the moving force of Will, into smaller and smaller segments until nothing remains but a non-point of consciousness, a void of pure awareness. From this place of pre-existence and pre-form, the awareness of Stalking Rose moved between Northeast and Southeast on the doubled Medicine Wheel. If observation were possible without changing both observer and observed, which it isn't, one might witness infinitesimal dots of black light, blinking off and on. There was always a danger in these deep realms that the medicine healer would not be able to re-manifest, return to form. To lessen the risk, she had left Abréu in the North position across from Little Mynx to keep their energy charge high; and she agreed to the request of Gavriel Navarro's spirit self to accompany her in the smoking of the windigo.

Although he could not vocalize at these levels and had no working experience with the Medicine Wheel, he had been trained by Amazon shamans in his early twenties long before he became a poet, and she recognized his pure soul. Abréu was right. The trapped spirit of Alain Dexter had no one else to turn to but Gavriel on the physical plane. His sexual energy, which is the creative Source, was beyond depleted; he was, literally, killing himself with every screw. A Jungian might say, it was his animus, male energy, not the anima, which heterosexual men gravitate toward, that needed replenishing. And although the concentrated turmoil of the windigo at his head and shoulders was thinning, she was nowhere near the core of it.

"We are working outside the time-space realm," she said to Gavriel in silent tongue. He stood, metaphorically, slightly behind and to the left of Stalking Rose, not unlike a medical student observing a doctor on his rounds. "What this means is, the adjustments we're making to Alain's energetic body may take effect in what appears to be his past— or yours. It's in the past where the damage begins and builds up, like scar tissue."

She felt a cool ripple along her left side that signaled Gavriel's understanding. Alain's spirit self remained in the cardinal East, protected by Abréu and Little Mynx.

"I'm going to circle the windigo now," she said, "moving closer in a spiral so that you can feel what it's made from. What I take in as knowing, you will receive too. It may not be retrievable when you return to your body self, but the knowledge will be fully stored, just like a data bank—and when you need it, it will be there."

The feelings of compression increased as she approached the dense, swirling cloud of energy. She had never scuba dived, but from what divers had described about descending into deep ocean, the comparison seemed apt.

The snapping, biting, salivating sounds were meant to unsettle her; she ignored them. Bertha Spotted Turtle sometimes called windigo the gaping maw because of the way it swam around, open, nothing but mouth, sucking up blame, shame, repression of the senses—and stirring up new trouble if it couldn't find enough of the old.

Stalking Rose made a few direct dives through the densest pockets of windigo, which felt like swimming into a high-pressure spray of razor blades. The screeching sounds alone would destroy a physical being with a force millions of times stronger than the vaporization of an atomic bomb.

Exiting the far side of windigo, rattled but unharmed, she felt a tap on her left shoulder. Gavriel Navarro, conveying the sense of his bodily self, moved a hand over a strangely speckled area of windigo that Stalking Rose had not noticed. It flapped and hung outside the cloud like an extra growth of skin. She'd never seen anything like it—not fully windigo but not free-moving energy either.

She peered more closely and requested clarification. Had it been pure chaotic energy, she would have demanded, and by law, it would have been obligated to cooperate. *A gathering, the best of . . .*

"The best of what?" It expressed the same again, as if the thought trail simply could not bring words any further.

The best of . . .

She turned to Gavriel. "Do you know about this gathering? Does it make sense to you?"

He nodded. His brows came together; beads of sweat popped out on his forehead, and while physical expressions of the spirit self are only symbolic, even Elsie with her anti-*wasichu* biases, would have recognized the strenuous effort Gavriel Navarro put forth to say, "Yes, I was there."

<hr>

I sat at my desk in the Brougham College Faculty of English with the afternoon light at my back, a mountain of envelopes and parcels in front of me. It was a Saturday morning, my first time in the office since Carolyn's funeral at St. George's Anglican in Nipigon. Over four hundred people had attended, and in the week that followed, I came to appreciate how much she had protected me. I felt like a walled city whose levees had been breached: all the phone calls, emails, deliveries of flowers and balloons, people I hardly knew showing up at all hours with casseroles, fruit baskets, veggie trays and cookies. Carolyn would have received all of their kindness with kindness. I just wanted them to stop.

I sorted through the envelopes and small parcels and considered throwing them all, unopened, into a Dumpster, but Nature is cruel and a campus is a village. Some rogue wind would lift those expressions of caring and scatter them at the feet of faculty and staff, and forever prove the cold, cold heart of Professor Alain Dexter.

Among the small parcels was a 9" x 12" bubble wrap envelope from Phoenix, Arizona. An address label identified the senders as Dr. Steven and Marie Coulthard. It took me a moment to place the name: Steve. Ginny's older brother.

I opened the envelope and pulled out a black Moleskine journal. A single sheet of folded stationery came out with it, along with a business card. Steve had become a dermatologist.

He introduced himself in the letter, acknowledging that it had been a long time, fifteen years, to be precise, since Ginny's death. His wife had caught the Moyers episode, and they were happy to know that I'd made it as a writer; he hoped I was well. So this wasn't about Carolyn.

I continued reading. Steve was executor to his father's estate; his mother had passed four years earlier. Going through his dad's files, he'd come across the journal I'd given Ginny and thought I might like to have it. He hadn't been sure of the identities of Sugarbean and Peppercorn in the inscription, but there'd been an invitation tucked in the back inside envelope addressed to Mistress V. Coulthard and Mister A.C. Dexter. It's funny, Steve wrote. I can't remember anyone referring to Ginny as Mistress V. It must have been quite a gig, and I hope you were able to attend.

Apart from being slightly faded, the journal was in good shape. Our luggage had been in the trunk of the Honda that day; I had no recollection of how Ginny's belongings found their way to her family.

Every authentic Moleskine contains a manila folder in the back inside cover. I pulled out a small square vellum envelope and from that the card that invited us, during our week at Hayden Lake, to a Circularity of Glosas.

The phrase meant nothing to me. I'd been teaching poetry for eight semesters, which included lectures on sonnets, sestinas and ghazals and had never heard—no, that wasn't true. If a circularity of glosas meant nothing, I wouldn't have come up with the sudden defense that I lectured on every other poetic form except glosas.

Something warned me to stop right there. Past is past; I'd just lost my wife. What did I hope to—

I opened the Moleskine. The back half of the journal was blank; the front pages were filled with drafts of glosas in Ginny's hand. My own hands started to shake while I turned to the final entry. My vision blurred, my stomach heaved and pitched, and I recalled what Ginny said when I came out of the shower, that final morning.

"You bastard, how could you do this to me?"

The first four lines came from Edgar Allan Poe's poem, "Coliseum". I had titled my glosa, "Unbreaking Fine Threads". Unlike Ginny's, mine had no scratch-outs or revisions. The handwriting of the final four stanzas was mine; the opening quatrain wasn't. My verses had been scribed with ball point pen, "Coliseum" was clearly in fountain pen. But none of those details tore at my flesh and spirit with as much brutality as the glosa itself:

Unbreaking Fine Threads

Not all our power is gone—not all our fame—
Not all the magic of our high renown—
Not all the wonder that encircles us—
Not all the mysteries that in us lie—
—"The Coliseum", Edgar Allan Poe

In dark pre-dawn I heard you creeping in—
no, I speak kind; you stumbled, crashing
the umbrella stand, that wedding gift unfit for
bumbershoots collapsed in spaceless entryways.
Old habit bade me leap: you freaking, no-good son—
but something stayed my hand and frame.
"Remain!" it spoke, a voice so firm I dared not
question, while fumes arose from me and
curled to ceiling height, a strange refrain:
not all our power is gone—not all our fame.

The kitchen light, the freezer door, then microwave;
how readable you are from this vast promontore
of stern and feckless view. I stay at home and
slap with angry trowel a sodden clay to cracks
of this relationship that crumbles from a dearth
of moisturing; my fierce determined frown
to harridan it leads where once I'd been
your sugar bean and you my peppercorn,
we've shredded our affinity to clown.
Not all the magic of our high renown

Can bridge the damage of your faithless
roving eye—did I not try to fill your lonely
crevices of expectation? "Refrain!" What?
The voice again comes scolding me as if
the steps ascending to this crumpled bed
were innocent, and I thrill-seeking devious.
Whose side, I shout, take you, oh fiend, oh

patron saint of treachery? Say what, you slur
and stare as if a horror were now obvious,
not all the wonder that encircles us.

You fall upon the feral bed we shared
until the one who gave you voice appeared
and gifts we thought were provident divided
us. Cleave not, the priest in Fiji said, ambiguous,
before we walked a bed of coals, mad newlyweds.
Fare well. It is, I see, no worthy sacrifice to die
for life it is that reconciles and ties the tiny
threads of love in capillary flow. The clot that
stopped my heart and brain will ne'er belie
not all the mysteries that in us lie.

"There is nothing more that we can do here," Stalking Rose said to
Gavriel Navarro, whose spirit essence had accompanied her to the
interior of the double Medicine Wheel. "If we stay too long and too
close to the stories of another, they can pull us in, begin to feed from
our own unfinished business. We have remained too long already."

Gavriel Navarro seemed mesmerized by the cluster of repressed
energy known as the windigo. It swarmed like an angry nest of hornets
around Alain Dexter's head and shoulders; extending appendages,
driving blades into his heart; it organized into claw-like strips and tore
at his intestines. The sick unity that masquerades as awareness,
intelligence and reason had been dealt a mortal blow, and was fighting
back. Windigo does not want us to remember, and when we do, it
works furiously to create new versions of the story to support its
continued existence.

The man looked up as if to say, "I have seen enough."

"Good, and so we will leave," Elsie Stalking Rose said. "You are
going to feel a sense of backing away, slowly, at first, and then
accelerating to warp speeds, as if something is pulling you from the back
of your shirt through universes and multiple realities that seem to go on

and on. Keep your gaze relaxed and lowered; make no attempt to focus on the peripheral blur, even if something catches your eye or appears to be flying across your flight path. Illusion is strong here, and whatever you see, it is only your past."

He conveyed his understanding by means of a tug at Stalking Rose's heart. Then he gave her a rose. She smiled. Aah, yes, Abréu had said you are a poet.

And so she began her own acceleration, paying no attention to the horrors of her youth, the injustices and tragedies she'd witnessed as a police officer and among her own people, all of which flew by her, clamouring for attention. They were not reality; they were temporary values apportioned to the light, sound, colour, harmony that is Manitou, Great Spirit, All That Is. From no-time, they decelerated to the borderlands of time-space, known to First Nations medicine as Dreaming Awake.

She and Gavriel landed in a desolate expanse of what appeared to be a no-man's land. The ocher, burnt and raw siennas of the landscape resembled the canvases of Georgia O'Keeffe, and the sunless sky, an indeterminate shade of gray-white, pulsed like the surface of an enormous fish eye. Here, they resembled their physical selves, for it was, quite literally, the place of self-in-potential, sometimes known as Crossroads. She scanned Gavriel and found him to be remarkably whole, considering.

"Are you all right?" she asked.

"I believe so." He looked down and ran his hands along his arms and upper legs, as if to reassure himself. "You said that the knowledge I received while we . . . while you broke apart the . . ."

Stalking Rose smiled. "Don't worry about trying to find the right words. There are none."

He looked relieved. "You said that I would be able to remember."

"That is so. Everything you observed in the nations of the doubled Wheel will be available to you, as you need them. You do not have sufficient energy stores yet to direct your Knowing, but this will come in your future. Much depends on how you handle the reparation of Alain Dexter, for when we heal another, we heal ourselves."

"Will you and I meet again?"

"Of that, I have no doubt. As an old priest, a dear friend of mine, used to say, the harvest is ready, but the workers are few."

"And will I know how—"

"Yes. Now, I must leave you." Stalking Rose placed her open hand over his heart. "May the warm winds of Heaven blow softly upon your house, Gavriel Navarro. May the Great Spirit Manitou bless all who enter there. May the tracks of your moccasins lead you to happiness, and the trail you leave bring others to theirs. My heart is full for having met you. *Wachyia.* So speaks Stalking Rose."

And with that, he vanished from her Dreaming Awake, as did Abréu of Valletta and the multitudes who'd accompanied them when she returned to the deep woods. The only proof that remained of the presence of the old *voyageur* was a turkey feather lying at the North position of Wisdom, across from Little Mynx.

⁂

Our bodies, when you come right down to it, are nothing more than cleverly designed shock absorbers. That was where I landed after reading my own word-by-word account of Carolyn's death and my own behaviour, fifteen years before the event. Did I remember that the opening line of my glosa had been whispered to me moments after Ginny and I made love for the last time, and again on the staircase, the night my wife died? Hell, yeah, now I remembered! If this were a Poe story, people would have loved it—Ginny would have loved it. If she hadn't been my girlfriend, horrified by my poetic prophecy, she'd have been thrilled by the sudden reappearance of her Moleskine that backed up the *Eureka* theories: *My God, Alain, can't you see? The plots of God are perfect; the universe is a self-contained, closed system, and so is each one of us. We are the Prime Cause and Prime Movers of our life.* But in reality, horrific plots are not welcome. The events we can't find uses for, that we can't fit neatly onto shelves of perception get dragged out onto the curb, hopefully to be picked up in the night by a neighbour or a Good Will truck, doesn't matter who, just so long as we never have to look at the unexplainable again.

So life went on. I cleaned up my behaviour: no more sleeping with students, caterers, readers and fans. I delivered four semesters of tried and true lectures to eager young minds; I turned down all requests for speaking engagements beyond a fifty-mile radius, which, living on the north shore of Lake Superior where sturgeons and wolverines couldn't care less, calmed my life considerably.

But then I got a phone call from a major New York publishing house. After being broadsided by e-books and social media, mainstream houses were finally getting their act together. Someone on their editorial staff had been following my YouTube presence and my book sales at Brougham College Press, and decided that poetry, dead in the water since Walt Whitman, could bring in big money again. Not only did they offer a seven-figure advance for previously unpublished work, they offered to spruce up my website, set up a Facebook profile, a Twitter account and all the other promotional bells and whistles that created (and could there be a more hideous phrase?) "authorial buzz".

Eighteen months of nothing-too-terrible-happening had made of me a pragmatist. I hadn't scratched a word of new poetry for years; the few dregs that didn't make it into my published collections deserved not to make it. If poetry were food, mine was about as appealing as the toast crumbs that accumulate in the top drawer of a single guy's kitchen.

So, because I was bored, tired of grieving and at my core, as ambitious as I'd been at twenty-four, I retrieved the Moleskine from a Rubbermaid storage bin in the basement and slapped together a collection of seventeen glosas, along with a witty foreword about the form's origin and structure. And because I'm not a total boob, I acknowledged my friend, the late Ginny Coulthard, as the original author; I even dedicated the book, "To G.C." and hoped that her only surviving family member, Dr. Steve Coulthard, was earning enough as a dermatologist that he wouldn't come after me for royalties.

He didn't. Looking back, a lawsuit would have been a piece of cake.

My new publishers loved *Dead to Rights: A Circularity of Glosas.* Within five days of my emailing the manuscript, the book was live and on-line, available in print and e-reader editions with massive shipments on their way to bookstores around the world. I won't burden you with the details of the promotional campaign—it was aggressive and murderous, authorial testicle squeezing at its finest—but by the spring of 2012, I had 1.7 *million* fans on my Facebook page.

By mid-June, though I was still trying to figure out Timeline, I had begun to post a few poems on Facebook, dregs with aftershave and accompanying photos, because my personal EMA, Editorial & Marketing Assistant assigned by the publisher, said that I should maintain an active social media presence to keep the Likes and comments coming. They'd be gleaning reader testimonials for my next book from those comments.

I was sitting on my back deck in a pair of boxers with my iPad, posting a new Facebook banner photo of Brougham College at sunset when I got a friend request from someone named Ginny Coulthard. I felt a minor jolt, but names are not unique; I share mine with a radio broadcaster in Quebec and a half dozen other minor Wiki presences. I clicked Confirm Friend Request, and in the next instant, a text box popped up in the lower right of my screen. The message read:

Hey, Peppercorn, remember me? I've downloaded Dead to Rights, *and I'm wondering why you didn't include the 18th glosa. Edgar and I are kinda disappointed. Hope all's well. Much love, Sugarbean.*

CHAPTER 7

CROSSROADS

In the mossy deep woods of towering pines and cedar, of maple, larch, white and silver birch—what northern Canadians call, with no irony, "bush"—it is either dark or twilight. According to the wrist watch in Elsie Kalahash's backpack, twenty-two minutes had passed since she'd last instructed Little Mynx to throw kindling onto the fire, to raise white smoke. And yet, the four-foot high mound of green sticks and grass was nearly depleted. Little Mynx sat, nodding off in her South position to the left of Alain Dexter's bare feet.

"I'm awake!" Jenah-Rae sat up with a jerk, then slapped a hand over her mouth and looked with wide, frightened eyes at the comatose man she was supposed to be guarding.

"It's all right," Elsie said. "We've completed the smoking. Whether our friend chooses to return or move onto the Good Blue Road is up to him. By the way, how long was I gone?"

"You mean like, where I couldn't see you? Omigod, hours. I tried to count how many times you signaled for more grass on the fire, but I lost track after 148. I was worried I'd run out, and you never told me what to do if that happens."

"What would you have done?"

Jenah-Rae looked around, taking in the corduroy layers of brown against green against brown against blackness. "I'd have stayed here and kept the fire going with whatever was nearby."

"That would have been the right thing to do. Now I need you to help me move him. He has spent long enough in the East."

Elsie loosened the space blanket at his shoulders so that she could grab hold of his armpits; Jenah-Rae took his feet. Together they shifted Alain Dexter's body from a north-south polarity to east-west. He lay now where Little Mynx had sat for hours, or for twenty-two minutes, depending on which thought trails the mind selected.

He was still inert and displayed no vital signs. But Stalking Rose knew from personal experience that the absence of pulse and respiration are not proof of death; at times, they are proof of fierce determination when the pulses of life retreat deeply inward to meet, like a council of elders, at the crossroads of thought and matter. As for the windigo, if they were still around, she ignored them. Negative loves negative but has no power without attention.

The fire had settled to an ashy bed of coals. Elsie picked up a few pieces of deadwood and threw them into the embers. "Now, Little Sister, you and I are going to find something to eat."

"Both of us? Shouldn't someone stay here?"

Elsie heard what Jenah-Rae had not said. *There are bears in these woods . . . and wolves and coyotes and snakes.* The teenager had not noticed, nor would she have understood the turkey feather lying in the Wheel's North position. One day, that feather would make fine ceremony in welcoming a new medicine woman onto her path.

"Look up at the sky, Little Mynx, and tell me what you see."

The girl tipped her head back to gaze at the patch of blue that mirrored the size of the clearing. "I see birds. Large birds . . . turkey vultures, circling." She looked at Elsie with alarm. "Are they waiting for him?"

"In a way. The buzzard is the Eagle of the South and carries powerful medicine. If our Mr. Dexter chooses death again, the four-legged, the creeping and the flying nations will receive their signal and do all that is necessary. Our presence would only disturb things."

But he's totally helpless.

Elsie ignored Jenah-Rae's silent protest. Someday, she would learn that "helpless" was the most insidious lie of the *wasichu.*

As they headed northward toward a patch of blueberry bushes Elsie hadn't visited in years, she said to Jenah-Rae, "Can you pick up a signal out here?"

"A signal." She wrinkled her nose in confusion. "You mean, like a . . . signal?"

"Yeah, you have your iPhone, don't you?"

"Uh-huh."

"I'd like you to google the name, Gavriel Navarro."

No one had ever called me Peppercorn except Ginny, and Sugarbean was my goofy term of endearment for her; both died when she died. I leaped back from the patio table as if someone had thrown scalding hot tar at me and stared at the iPad from a distance of six feet. It was a cruel joke; I must have blurted something in a drunken state to one of my many one-night stands.

Slowly, I crept back to my computer, clicked the Chat options to Offline, and visited my newest FB friend's Timeline. The banner photo was of her and me in front of the cabin at Hayden Lake, arms around each other, a couple of grinning kids in love, Ginny holding up two fingers behind my head. We'd used my timer and tripod. That was back in pre-digital days; she hadn't lived long enough to see the photo. I recognized her profile pic, a studio head shot, and she was as pretty as I remembered: blue-gray eyes, light brown curly hair that just made you want to crumple handfuls of it and kiss her stupid; a wide, winning, open smile. There were no shades of Chucky the Clown in this impossibility, no fangs or evil eye.

But reading her personal info, I began to crack: employed at Brougham College, Professor of English Literature; studied English at BC; lives in Nipigon, Ontario; hometown, Sarnia. In other words, this was Ginny Coulthard if she had lived and attained her ideal life . . . most of which ended up being my life. My interior vision crossed and blurred to black, red and swimmy geometric designs. I could barely focus as I clicked on the message feature, to read again her taunting question about why I had not included the glosa, "Unbreaking Fine Threads" with the quatrain from Edgar Allan Poe.

The simple truth was, I'd been too ashamed. Posting a blow-by-blow poem of a failed marriage and a wife's death that might have occurred anyway, but was certainly not helped by years of living with an unfaithful husband. And if I had included "Unbreaking Fine Threads", could I have let the poem stand, or would I have felt obligated to utter disclaimers? *I wrote this in 1995, years before I met my wife, and yes, coincidentally, in 2010, I came home blind drunk.*

No way. Anything I'd have said would have called attention to the most deplorable parts of me. I was a professor with a Ph.D., a best-selling author, a celebrity!

Typing my reply, I hit the keyboard letters so hard the table rattled. "Where the fuck do you come off, impersonating a dead woman on FB? I'm going to report, defriend and block you!!!" Hitting the multiple exclamation points felt both ridiculous and satisfying.

She replied right away. "Don't be angry. I love the book, I really do, and thank you for the dedication."

"Stop it! You are not Ginny!" I shouted aloud, backing away again from the computer. She continued to write, a sentence or two popping up at a time.

"You've never owned up to the party, Alain. The Circularity of Glosas was real, and it's everything. All those poets, philosophers, your favourite novelists. You could have let the Third Place change your life."

"But you never owned up to it," I said, alone in my back yard, to the computer screen. "Our last argument was about the party. You claimed it never happened."

"I know that I was in denial. I wish I could change that, but I can't. It was my day to die. We block so much of what flows from our imagination, allowing only the narrowest of thought streams. It's just like Poe said in *Eureka*—"

"Ginny, stop, please!" I couldn't take anymore. I grabbed the hair at my temples, squeezed my eyes shut and sank to the floor of the deck, like an overwhelmed little boy who can't bear another word of his parents' fighting.

I rolled into a ball and sobbed. I rocked back and forth, keening, not caring who in my upper middle class, suburban campus neighbour-hood heard. And during that massive release, while I retched and wailed, images started to form—not just images but variations of movement, intention, direction, event. My "self", or perhaps a better word, my presence, shifted to become the tubular space inside a hollow reed; the events I was witnessing from the past were fibers of the reed being pulled away. The future was among them too: infinite filaments, each of which represented a possible or potential event with outcomes, peeling from the reed while I watched, dispassionate observer, from my space-seat at the center.

Then my vision shifted again, and I saw two specific threads taking on greater vitality, depth, and dimension. From my vantage, they extended outward like curving uphill paths—crossroads. I could take one, or I could take the other.

Following the fiber-event to the left, I returned to my iPad, defriended and blocked the sicko fake Ginny who'd found a way to torment me with details that she/he had obviously researched. Fueled by a massive erection that appeared from nowhere, I penned a long sarcastic poem shaped like a pair of boobs, saved it as a draft, then calmly, almost studiously, went inside to put on a T-shirt, jeans and lumber jacket. I gathered my iPhone, wallet and car keys, and drove to Valletta Falls where I used my phone to photograph my toes hanging over the edge of the cliff. I posted the poem, "I Once Knew a Woman" on Facebook with the accompanying image and waited long enough to see the first few hundred likes and comments before taking a step forward.

Observed, registered, done.

I "turned" then to the fiber at the right, a pale golden pathway, identical in essence to the left-hand path. In this option, I allowed for the possibility that relationships survive bodily death, and that my beloved Ginny had somehow found a way to use cyberspace to communicate her love to me. As before, I entered the house, but this time, I retrieved the original Moleskine journal and my new hardcover edition of *Dead to Rights: A Circularity of Glosas* and brought them outside to my iPad.

I had done enough research when preparing the manuscript to know that PK (Patricia) Page, who'd attended the party at Hayden Lake and published her own collection of glosas, died in 2010 at the magnificent age of 93. The only one of the seventeen writers and thinkers in Ginny's glosas who was still alive in the literal sense was a person I didn't recall meeting at the party. But there'd been so many, and I'd spent a lot of time on the porch, slugging back beer.

I knew the bilingual shaman-poet had a website because I'd contacted him to obtain permission to use his quatrain, "Certain

Things are Priceless" in Ginny's glosa, which she had entitled, appropriately, "Siege". This time, I logged onto Skype, searched for Gavriel Navarro, and sent him a request to connect. I also typed in a message:

Gavriel, I understand that you and I attended the same party years ago, with a lot of famous people. Some weird things are going on, and I wonder if you'd have time to talk.

I went inside to get some lemonade, and when I returned, the Skype phone was ringing. I answered, "Hello."

"Hi, Alain, it's Gav."

❦

Being not quite satisfied, Elsie added a few leaves of salt grass to the wild sage, thyme, mint, berry broth, also known as medicine tea. She tasted again and muttered, "Perfect."

Jenah-Rae, who'd refused to snare a rabbit for the stew, sat with her knees pulled to her chin, watching life force gather around the man lying east-weat. His clothes had dried, and they had dressed him. He wasn't breathing yet, but life force returns first as a whispery steam; then the pulses kick in.

The central fire of the Ancient Heart, Sacred Zero, was an ordinary cooking fire now and their only light, casting a perfect circle against the blackness of the woods. The rumbling Tourbillon in the background assured Jenah that, yes, rivers too have moods and preferences, and the *wasichu* had been not at all to its taste. On the other hand, as accompanying thunder to Elsie Kalahash's lightning, Alain Dexter would bring powerful medicine to many, and Little Mynx, as Medicine Wheel elder-in-training, would have her hands full in bringing them together.

"You think?" she said to the river in silent tongue. "Watch this." She shifted on her butt, and with precisely the right amount of teenaged Little Sister enthusiasm, exclaimed, "Elsie, Elsie, look!"

Elsie set down her stirring stick and gazed across the fire at the very instant that Alain C. Dexter opened his eyes.

94

EIGHTEEN MONTHS LATER

Borgarnes, Iceland, had never hosted such a prestigious event as the Fifth Annual PES^{2}A^{3}C. The Birki Skóga Inn was booked to the rafters, and Asti Fridleifsdotter had never seen her mother so happy, chatting up eight hundred of the world's best pickings of economists, scientists and artists. Asti stood in the wings of the outdoor tent they'd pitched in a fallow oat field for the event, and reviewed her Mistress of Ceremony cue cards. PES^{2}A^{3}C, pronounced, thankfully, without the superscripts, as Pea Sack, stood for Poe's Economic and Scientific Summit Aspiring to Abundance through Artistry Conference. The next presenter, standing to her right in an open white shirt and khakis, gave her a playful wink.

"Ready?" Alain Dexter said.

She smiled back at him. "Ready."

The best-selling poet professor, one of the biggest draws at the three-day event, had rocked the publishing industry the previous year with his decision to pull the first edition of *Dead to Rights: A Circularity of Glosas* and sign with a new, forward-thinking UK press to produce a restructured second edition with eighteen glosas, based on the Native American Medicine Wheel. The outrage and attempts to litigate in New York were huge; in the end, Alain allowed the large house to sell its remaining physical inventory and withdraw the e-book and rights to future work. The inventory sold out in fourteen hours.

Gavriel Navarro sat in the second row of the audience beside PESAC's principal funder, Virginia Coulthard-Azzar, wife of an Egyptian economist and mother of seven-year-old Allen Charles, who'd just flown in from Dubai. When the time was right, Gavriel would introduce her to Alain Dexter who would see before him his own Ginny, twenty years on, and startle at the resemblance. The hemp bracelet she wore, woven by her son, would strike him as impossible coincidence, but all things coincide and nothing is impossible.

The most important feature, however, of Professor Dexter's presentation, due to begin in moments, was the row of chairs at the front, marked Reserved, that, to the ordinary eye, appeared empty. Among the honoured guests sitting in the row were PK Page, Epictetus, John Keats and Rumi. Seated between Charles Dickens and Giacomo Casanova was a pale American man with longish wavy hair, a moustache, and a penetrating fire in the eye.

Asti Fridleifsdotter introduced Alain C. Dexter. When the applause died down and the author looked out at the audience, he met the eye of that dark-haired man, who replied with a nod and a quietly uttered, "Eureka."

POSTSCRIPT

LET ME BE THAT HAND
by Alain C. Dexter

I watched you writing last night, pale
hand in the light of a crescent moon
a kerosene lantern at the window of
the cabin you'd invited me to share.

I was on my way to meetings—no, I
lie—I trod through snow to where I knew
I'd find you, doing what you love, heart
taking shape, poetic on a page.

I should have been there. I could have
been propped on that great feather bed,
feet bare, penning my own prose with
ink that flows sleek, black and shiny
like good ink ought to flow.

That my throat and pen are running dry
creeps dangerous close to cliché, but true.
I'm pulling out old tricks, while the flow
upon your Moleskine pages—and I do
see them—runs fresh and new.

The light dusting of snow at the window
I ache to brush away…with this hand.

The hand that would have held the one
now writing at the scarred wooden table,
wrapping fingers around your cherished
palm, lifting it to moist lips.

Instead, this hand hangs fisted at my side,
curled snug and dry in its own stupidity.

Yes, I am surrounded by the glory we saw
coming. Shapely forms compete to place their
name cards next to mine, inviting me to feast
when the speeches and the tables are cleared.

They are convinced I pour my words to some
elusive woman; they battle like wolverines
to displace her. Only you see the truth of who
writes to whom and you stand by me anyway,
spirited, alone, invisible in my presence while
I kick at the chambers that contain you, my
beloved, accusing and confusing these locked
doors with you. Here is my last confession:

Not only did I see you at the window, I came
to your door. I knew that with light pressure
of my thumb upon the latch, the door would
open—you never lock anything, but when I
reached out my arm, you looked up and
your face clouded with confusion. That
hand on the door, though you knew it was
coming—how could it be mine, after all
the pushing and slamming I'd done?

I stood silent and still, long enough
for you to return your attention to the
words you were penning. You lifted
a hand absently to your cheek.

In that moment, in your full presence,
I whispered, let me be that hand.

Siege: A Glosa

by Ginny Coulthard, edited by Alain C. Dexter

There are certain things I will not tell you;
you will find your way among the roses I write
because certain redundancies are not given to silence
or the sorrows of the soul, or the pleasures of the body.

—"Certain Things are Priceless", Gavriel Navarro

Our bus broke down last night on the outskirts
of Montségur, that castled sugar loaf where dualists
held out until the last of them was set to flame and
choice of thought once more was laid aside in favour
of the true. I would have texted you had it not been
for the shepherd who assisted us; a Basque, he drew
me to his mountain heights, we left the others with
their bedrolls and their blogs, we hardly spoke, his
grin was slow and shy, and very soon I knew
there are certain things I will not tell you.

I can say this: the sheep that break the fences
of the prohibitions that protect a sense of dignity
that's false are God's true creatures, and the others?
Well, we've all been fleeced and sold for meat and
cheese; I cannot count myself as rebel when it suits
me, nor is the reflex jolt of recognition proof of right
or wrong or better. Yet I must speak of disappointment
as I see it, every time the falling short becoming more
predictable, so you'll pardon me, I hope, this flight;
you will find your way among the roses that I write.

And when the space between your words and mine
dissolves and fades to dim, I will not plow you under
nor make of you a gilt-edged memory to swap with
buddies at the lonely-hearted food court. Our life spans
were extended for much more than this, and so I'll
take my sandwiches and canvas sack of impudence
in search of signs that say don't touch, abandoned
mines and circling, pointless stairs. No more a fitful
subjugate, I happily discard the weight of our events
because certain redundancies are not given to silence

And this was never meant to be a sorry tale. That's what
we were making, you and I—endurance and longevity
as ends are bleeding bores—so celebrate we should that
in the nick of time, the Peugot on the hairpin road becomes
instead an accident to fling us from the factual, contractual,
and when I take that shepherd's hand, I'll turn to free
you from your wreckage. The dusty road to Compostelle
has many cul-de-sacs not on the map; it doesn't mean
we're lost. The siege is done. We never gave up liberty
or the sorrows of the soul, or the pleasures of the body...

By Gavriel Navarro

Certain Things are Priceless: A Navarrete Quatrain

There are certain things that I write
that arise beyond the world where I move
in the course of time, if it actually happens
I'm dropping accurately through that hole

There are certain beauties that are not redundant
and so I plunge into that cave silently, where
I feel sure of myself, without resistance and it's
hard not to surrender to her charms and shadows ...

There are certain sadness and certain pleasures
where I exist in an infinite well of inspiration, captive
always evolving, breathing deeper upon your breast
raw and simple like that flower just flourishing ...

There are certain things I will not tell you;
you will find your way among the roses I write
because certain redundancies are not given to silence
or the sorrows of the soul, or the pleasures of the body ....

AUTHOR'S NOTE:

Gavriel Navarro is a Spanish-born poet, musician and artist who grew up in Venezuela and England. After graduating with a degree in Fine Arts and Graphic Design, he spent eleven years in the Amazon as a hunter, an Eco-tourism guide and apprentice of shamanic wisdom. The multilingual Navarro now makes his home in Japan where he applies the lessons of his peripatetic life through film-making and transcendent poetry. He has published two volumes of a trilogy of verse: *The Wind and the Sea: Poems and Reflections on the Voyage of No Return,* and *Fire and Earth: Poems and Reflections on the Nature of Desire.*

You can find all eighteen glosas co-written by Alain C. Dexter, Ginny Coulthard, and a gathering of the finest poets, prose writers and philosophers throughout the centuries in the accompanying volume, *Dead to Rights: A Circularity of Glosas,* edited by Elaine Stirling, published by Greyhart Press.

Dead to Rights

A Circularity of Glosas

Alain C. Dexter